REPLACEMENT

THE WORTHINGS

NOELLE ADAMS

1

LOOKING AT AMBER HAS ALWAYS BEEN LIKE LOOKING IN A mirror.

I haven't seen her in nine years, so the experience is eerie, unfamiliar. She still has our natural hair—medium brown, straight, and shiny—while I started highlighting mine blond shortly after I left home. Her clothes are much more elegant and expensive than my faded jeans and leather jacket. But the green eyes, small nose, full lips, high cheekbones, curvy figure, and fair skin—all of it is exactly like mine.

There are a few minor differences, of course. I have a small scar at my temple from a fall off monkey bars when I was five. Amber's eyebrows are thinner and darker than mine, and her arms are more toned since I've been too scared and distracted to go to the gym lately.

But we're identical twins, and no one could ever tell us

apart.

Even our father would get us confused far too often.

He was a crappy dad in worse ways than that.

Amber stopped talking to me when I walked out the day I turned eighteen even though I repeatedly explained I was leaving him and not her. I begged her to come with me. She wouldn't give up on our father, which meant she gave up on me.

All my attempts to get in touch with her—before and after our dad died two years ago—went unanswered. Even the desperate, rambling voice mail I left her two months ago explaining that I have a stalker, and I'm scared, and I really need someone to trust was ignored.

Until two days ago. I got a letter forwarded from my previous PO box to my new one. Amber. She sent me a phone number and asked me to call.

She said she's sorry. She's not angry anymore. She wants to make up for things. She has an idea that might help us both.

I'm not sure there's anything left that could help me. The police won't do anything about Vince Montaigne, my stalker, until he makes a more direct threat, and he's got friends in the department anyway, including his best friend, Detective Curtis. *Having an admirer is different than having a stalker. Don't be melodramatic. Take it as a compliment.* That's what Detective Curtis told me with the most condescending smirk imaginable.

I can't trust the police. I can't trust anyone. I've had to move twice and quit my job. I never had many friends, and now I'm afraid to even go outside.

Amber is my twin sister, however. If I can trust anyone in the world, it's her.

So yesterday I bought a bus ticket from Houston to Atlanta and then another one from Atlanta to DC. I used cash for both since I'm convinced Montaigne has been able to track my credit card purchases. The tickets used up almost everything left in my bank account, but at this point, I don't even care.

Maybe I can at least make up with Amber before Montaigne kills me.

At two o'clock in the afternoon, she and I meet at a coffee shop in Georgetown.

Amber pulls back when I try to hug her, so we stare at each other instead.

"Hi, Jade," she says at last.

"Hi."

Jade and Amber Delacourte. Those are our names. The only thing that could make the names more ridiculous is the fact that our father was scion of a hundred-year-old jewelry dynasty.

Our dad was brilliant. An artist in precious metals and stones. But he was the world's worst businessman and gradually piddled away the entire Delacourte inheritance. The more money he lost, the more he drank and the meaner he became. By the time I turned eighteen, I'd had enough of cowering behind the locked door of my bedroom and putting up with his ruthless verbal attacks.

I moved halfway across the country with nothing more than a three-year-old car and the skill with jewelry my dad taught me. I didn't go to college, but I eventually got a job with a jeweler who never asked or cared how I came to learn the craft.

He never questioned the fact that I was uniquely talented and decidedly overqualified for the position he gave me. I mostly did repairs and the occasional custom piece for an engagement or anniversary. The job paid enough for a quiet, comfortable life, and that was all I was looking for back then.

Now I don't even care about comfort. My only dream is to be able to walk outside without constantly scanning my surroundings, searching for one face in particular.

We order our drinks and take a seat in a back corner with a clear view of the door so I can see everyone who comes in.

"I'm sorry, Jade." Amber's nails are beautifully manicured with elegant french tips. Her hair is pulled back in a sleek chignon. Her outfit is tailored trousers and a cashmere sweater—both in a lovely cream color I'd be constantly worried about spilling coffee on. Her purse and heels are deep red. Designer.

She always cared about the trappings of wealth more

than I did, and she hated our family's decline. When we were girls, she'd talk through all kinds of crazy fantasies about how we might one day regain our wealth.

Most of those daydreams involved latching onto a rich, handsome man.

"Wh-why are you sorry?"

There are any number of things she might apologize for, including pretending I don't exist for nine years, but what she says is a complete surprise. "I can't give you any money."

My lips part slightly. "I didn't ask you for money."

"I know. But I'm just saying. I wish I could give you something so you could start a new life and get away from that creep. But I can't. I don't have anything to give you."

Ever since I left home, I've kept to myself. Done my job. Gone home after work. Avoided any sort of intimate relationship. Been self-sufficient and pragmatic and more cynical than I was as a kid. No one would ever accuse me of being soft or vulnerable now, but even I can't match the cold bitterness of Amber's voice and expression.

Life hasn't been good to me. For the past seven months, it's been actively trying to kill me. But I suspect it's been even harder on Amber.

"I don't have any money," Amber adds, her voice brittle.

Despite my annoyance at her assuming I'm looking for a payout, I can't help but lower my eyes to Amber's designer clothes, shoes, handbag, and jewelry. Her purse alone almost certainly cost more than my car.

"The money is his," Amber explains, reading my expression correctly. "Not mine."

I wouldn't know anything about Amber's life now had I not regularly researched her online. She's shared absolutely nothing with me. But her current boyfriend is both wealthy and well-known. They've been living together in DC for at least a few months. They're engaged to be married.

William Worthing. That's his name. He has a family legacy as notorious as ours, but the Worthings have been much smarter with their money. They're wealthier than they were a hundred years ago, and they're known primarily for having a lot of very good-looking male heirs.

Amber lets out a breath and adjusts the large sunglasses that are resting on the top of her head. "If I ask him for money, I need a reason. He'll give me money to buy a piece of jewelry or a new car, but then he'll expect to see the necklace or the car. He may have money coming out of his ears, but he's going to want to see evidence of what I do with a pile of cash. I'm sorry, Jade. I simply can't give you any money."

That actually makes sense to me. I don't think she's lying. "As I said before, I'm not asking for money. I've been trying to reconnect with you for nine years. I'm not here for the money."

"I know. But I wanted you to know I'd give you some if I was able."

"Thank you. I appreciate that. I guess money might help, but it's not what I'm looking for. I just want to... feel safe again."

Seven months ago, I started getting red roses. One at a time. On my welcome mat. On the hood of my car. On the table where I always sat on weekend mornings in my favorite coffee shop.

At first I was confused and intrigued since aside from the occasional one-night stand with a stranger, I don't do any sort of relationship. Who would even notice me, much less give me roses like that?

After a couple of weeks, the roses continued but got creepier. They showed up on my desk at work. Inside my car. In my shopping cart at the grocery store when I left it for just a minute to grab something from another aisle.

I went to the police. They did nothing.

Then I started getting texts and phone calls. They weren't threats. They were asking about my day and what I was watching on television, as if we were on friendly terms. The police told me to change my phone number. I did, but soon the calls and texts began again. And this time they were scarier, using details from my daily routine that no one should know.

Since the cops weren't doing anything, I hired a private

investigator who was able to trace the calls and track the stalker.

Vince Montaigne. A wealthy but seemingly normal guy in his thirties. The week before I started getting the roses, he came into my jewelry shop to order a custom piece for his mother, and I met with him for about twenty minutes to get the details on what he wanted.

That was it.

That one encounter turned into this.

His family has money and a lot of connections in Houston, so my attempts to do something legally ran into nothing but dead ends. So I moved, subletting a cheap studio. Started using nothing but prepaid phones. Eventually quit my job and waited tables at a diner.

For almost a month, I could actually breathe, thinking I'd finally shaken him.

But then Detective Curtis showed up in the diner. I recognized him from my attempts to get the police to help. I'd always suspected he was friends with Montaigne because of the way he talked to me, but soon I knew it for sure.

The next day, Montaigne was sitting at a booth in the diner with a smirk on his face.

I went back to the kitchen and quit my job then and there, giving up a week's pay just to get out of there quickly. I hurried home, gathered up my stuff, and left my new apartment.

I got a room in a cheap, long-stay hotel that accepted cash and didn't care that I was giving them a fake name.

That was five weeks ago. I've been living on my savings ever since, not daring to get another job, but now my time and my money have run out. I have no other resources, and I'm too tired to try the same thing again.

So here I am with my sister, prepared to say I'm sorry. I love you. And goodbye.

Amber says, "I understand you need to feel safe again. I have an idea."

I don't have much hope in any of her ideas. Amber was always creative but supremely impractical. I was always the one to get us out of trouble. But there's a flutter of feeling in my chest, simply from the fact that she's trying.

She wants to help.

No one but me and the occasional passing stranger has tried to help me in so long.

"What is it?" I ask, scanning the family walking in the front door to make sure they aren't suspicious.

"I want to get away, and you need to hide. So why don't you take my place?"

I'm not sure the extent of my surprise can be accurately described. I blink. Freeze. Spend way too long processing what she just said and trying to wrap my mind around it. "Wh-what?"

"Take my place. Pretend to be me. Then I can get away and your stalker will never be able to find you."

"But... How can... But... wh-*what*?"

"We look enough alike to pull it off. You can wear my clothes and take my stuff. We'll go to a salon around here where they don't know me so they can shape your eyebrows, redo your highlights, and style your hair better. You can say you felt like going blond. Everyone will focus on the change in hair and not on anything else."

"You're crazy! You must be crazy. It's... insane."

"Maybe. But I think we can do it."

"You live with someone, don't you? He's not going to be fooled."

"Sure he will. He's not there half the time anyway."

"You really think I'm going to have sex with your boyfriend just to—"

"He's not my boyfriend. Not for real. And we don't have sex."

That surprises me enough to halve the momentum of my initial astonishment. "Wh-what?"

"He's not my boyfriend. It's a business arrangement. He's desperate to prove himself to his family. Getting the Delacourte brand into the Worthing fold will be a huge coup for him."

"So why not just sell what's left of the company? If he's desperate and rich, surely he'd pay."

"Yes. That's what he wanted initially. But I can't." She shakes her head, her perfectly painted lips turning down in a pout I remember from when we were kids. "Dad tied it up legally when he died. I'm not allowed to sell it."

Despite everything else, this isn't a surprise to me. Our father was always controlling, manipulative, untrusting of anyone—especially women. "Fucking bastard."

Amber doesn't rile up in defense the way she used to whenever I said anything negative about our dad. Instead, she looks faintly annoyed. "Be that as it may, it's the reality of the situation. So the only way I could get anything out of the damn company was to make this arrangement. A practical arrangement where we date, get engaged, and then get married. I was hoping it could just be for appearances, but he wanted to try it for real." Her mouth turns up with a flicker of disgust.

Ridiculously, I kind of feel bad for William Worthing in the face of Amber's clear contempt. "You don't want to try?"

"I'm not interested in that kind of relationship. So we're still trying, but the agreement is clear. When we marry and our assets are officially joined, he gets the Delacourte brand and I..."

"You get what?"

"The payout I deserve."

"So what's the problem? Why not wait it out until you're married? Surely it's not a long time."

"It's not, but I don't like him. He's controlling. He thinks he can tell me what to do and what not to do. I don't want to live with him anymore."

"But you still want your payout." It's a statement, not a question. I understand what's happening now.

Amber isn't interested in reconciling with me. Her priority isn't even saving me from danger.

She wants an easy escape from an awkward situation while still getting the money she thinks is hers.

It hurts. The weight of disappointment. But I've stopped expecting people to be good. Even my own family has done nothing but let me down.

"I deserve it. I stuck with Dad until the end, and you know exactly what I had to deal with. I'm owed *something*."

Transactional. That's what the relationship with our father was to her. She put in the time and effort, and she deserves to be paid for it.

"So just marry Worthing. You're engaged, right? Speed up the marriage and get your payout."

"I have to stay with him for at least four more months. We have a contract. I don't get anything unless I go through with the whole agreement."

"Are you sure? If it's a business arrangement to him, why would he care about shortening the length of time you're stuck together?"

"He wants it to at least look real. He thought maybe we could make it work, but even if we can't, he doesn't want anyone suspecting the whole thing is a ridiculous ruse.

He's got... issues with his family, and he wouldn't agree to it unless we made it look like a real relationship to the rest of the world."

"I guess that makes sense." I sip my coffee, my eyes on the front door, watching every single newcomer to make sure there's no sign of longish dark hair and wireframe glasses. "But it doesn't the change the fact that he's going to recognize that I'm not you."

"No, he won't. I just told you our relationship is not real."

"But he must know you have a twin sister—"

"He doesn't. I never told him about you."

I try not to wince from a stab of pain in my heart. "Okay. But I'm sure he ran some sort of background check on you—"

"Of course. But after you left, Dad was so mad he bribed some people to change the paperwork so there's no record of you."

"He *what*?" I didn't think it was possible for my father to hurt me like that again, but somehow he's managed it even from the grave.

"You betrayed him. You know how he was. So he made it like you never existed."

I'm having trouble breathing through this new blow, but I force myself to move on. "Even with the paperwork changed, someone could still look into our past and find out—"

"He ran a normal background check. It wouldn't have shown up there. He didn't send a whole team to investigate every detail of my past. I'm telling you, he has no idea that I have a sister. He's never going to suspect one is taking my place. Plus, he's gone half the time traveling for work, and when he's in town, he's at the office all day long. We go to some social stuff together as part of the ruse and sleep in the same bed, but that's it. If you wear my clothes and go through my daily routine, he'll have no clue."

The mention of the bed makes my spine stiffen. "You don't have sex with him?"

"No. We agreed we could if we both want to, but I've been saying I don't know him well enough yet. We kiss occasionally, but that's it. You're not going to have to fuck him. Or pretend you're in love with him. You just need to be there. Fill the empty space."

"What about your friends?"

"I don't have any real ones. Only some who act friendly but don't give a shit about me for real. I'm telling you, this can work."

It's a ridiculous idea. Utterly irrational. Without a prayer of succeeding.

But I'm starting to consider it. Amber desperately wants it. And if I'm living her life, then Montaigne will never find me.

I won't be me, but I'll be able to let out my breath at last.

Maybe I can actually do it.

"What will you do?" I ask her.

"I've squirreled some money away over the past few months, so I have enough to live on until the time of the contract runs its course. Then I can divorce him and be me again, and by then, maybe your stalker will have given up. If not, I can split the money with you so you'll have enough to go somewhere else and be someone different. Whatever you want."

"And you think this plan has the slimmest chance of succeeding?"

"I think so. But if it doesn't, so what? What exactly do you have to lose?"

Nothing. The answer to her question is nothing.

I'm twenty-seven years old, and I've lost everything that's ever meant anything to me. Even the last flimsy thread of my family.

I have absolutely nothing left to lose.

Several hours later, my heart is racing wildly as I step out of a chauffeured car in front of a fancy building in DC. My skin has broken out in a cold sweat, and I'm expecting at every moment for someone to loudly identify me as an impostor.

Fortunately, our trip to the salon ensured my hair and

face is perfectly styled and made up, and the clothes Amber was wearing earlier basically fit me, although the waistband on the pants is a lot snugger than I'd ever wear by choice and I'm having to struggle not to wobble in these ridiculously high heels.

I like cute clothes as much as anyone, but I've never been as style conscious as Amber, and lately I've barely been leaving home and not wearing anything but baggy sweats.

This is part of the role I'll be playing for the next four months at least, however. I'm going to have to get used to wearing Amber's clothes.

Maybe she'll have something slightly more comfortable in her closet.

I'm able to hold my expression composed and my mouth turned down in a reflection of Amber's pout. I keep my sunglasses on, even when I step inside the building, since I feel safer behind them.

"Good afternoon, Ms. Delacourte," the doorman says with a polite smile.

I nod in response and keep moving toward the security station guarding the private elevator that goes up to the penthouse apartment, which belongs to William Worthing.

"Hello, Ms. Delacourte," the guard says. "How are you today?"

"Fine. Thank you. How about you?" I smile at him

since he sounds so friendly. But, at his faintly surprised expression, I realize I've made a mistake. I absently pat my hair, which is pulled back in the smooth chignon like Amber wore, and step into the elevator.

"I'm good," the guard replies, his surprised expression fading. "I like your new hair."

I smile my thanks, relieved when the elevator doors slide shut, leaving me by myself.

While I was at the anonymous salon in the suburbs getting my hair, nails, and eyebrows done, Amber booked a last-minute appointment at her regular salon and asked for her hair to be highlighted blond. The result is close to my color, and now anyone who happens to check it out will see proof that Amber indeed got her hair done today.

At the coffee shop, we spent an hour going over the details of Amber's life so I'll be prepped for taking her place. She was clearly counting on me agreeing to the plan because she gave me a small notebook full of important information like her passwords, her normal schedule and routines, and details on the main people in her life. After the hair appointments, we met in the dressing room of a large department store where we swapped clothes and bags. Amber then called her car and driver to take me home and waited until the coast was clear and then took a taxi to wherever it is she's going.

She didn't tell me where that is. Knowing my sister, there's probably another man involved.

I would have thought William Worthing would be right up her alley. I've seen pictures of him. He looks like he's in his thirties—probably no more than ten years older than us. He's good-looking like all the Worthings. Strong features, slightly too-long brown hair, and an aura of focused intensity. He's certainly wealthy enough to satisfy Amber's daydreams, but she said he's controlling and bossy. Probably difficult to manipulate.

When I asked specifically, she swore he's not violent or abusive. She simply doesn't like him and doesn't want to deal with him for four more months.

I suppose it might be true, but I doubt she would have left had she not already had a man waiting in the wings.

At this point, Amber's rationale isn't the most important thing to me. I can deal with William Worthing and with whatever other mess is present in my sister's life.

At least no one is stalking or threatening to kill her.

Let Amber run off to some private island with her secret lover if that's what she wants. I can temporarily become Amber Delacourte.

And Jade can just disappear.

The penthouse apartment is astonishing.

It's huge and luxurious in a sleek, contemporary, minimalist style—with vast city views, white marble floors, black lacquer furniture, and lush white upholstery.

I put down Amber's shiny red designer bag and wander around the living area, dining room, and kitchen with my mouth open.

I wonder if they ever do normal things in this place—like eat lasagna or drink coffee. I'm absolutely certain I will end up slopping something on the pristine white sofa.

There's a single purple orchid on a console table and a slash of red paint on the black-and-white abstract painting above the marble fireplace. Otherwise, no color breaks the black, white, and silver room except the blue of the sky through the wall of windows.

I don't like the decor at all. It feels sterile, artificial.

I can't help wondering if the decor is Amber's doing or if it was like this when my sister moved in.

Maybe this is William's style rather than Amber's.

The apartment is dead silent. Amber mentioned there's a housekeeper named Greta, who comes in most days but doesn't live here. She must not be here right now. I walk around the entire place, taking note of what is in every room so I'll know my way around.

One door off the main hallway is locked. Maybe William's home office. I haven't seen one, and I can't imagine a man like him not having one.

Once I learn the layout of my new home, I go into the master bedroom, which is just as white, elegant, and luxurious as the rest of the home. I open every single drawer and investigate every corner, making sure I know where all Amber's clothes and belongings can be found.

She said she isn't having sex with William, but she clearly lives and sleeps in the master bedroom. All her clothes are in the closet, and all her makeup and hair supplies are in the glitzy bathroom.

It's strange to see a man's clothes—rows of tailored suits, polished shoes, ludicrously expensive watches—lined up in the huge closet across from Amber's. And even stranger to see male toiletries in the bathroom and books on Greek history and economic theory that are obviously not Amber's on one of the bedside tables.

It feels intimate. It makes me nervous.

Surely Amber wouldn't lie about having sex, but it's strange they're sleeping in the same bed. Maybe it's for appearances or maybe because William wanted to "try out" the relationship. A pair of Amber's earrings and an ivory-cased tablet are lying on the opposite night-stand next to the bed, so that's clearly the side she sleeps on.

William is evidently out of town all week—which will give me time to acclimate to my new role before I have to play a much more difficult part. Amber said William won't be hard to convince since he doesn't pay much attention to her anyway.

But still...

Even without sex being a factor, is there any way I'm actually going to be able to pull this off?

My stomach churns nervously at the thought of William returning from his business trip, but I force the anxiety to the back of my mind.

I'll have other challenges to tackle before then.

When I've familiarized myself with the apartment, I realize I'm hungry and find some leftover Thai food in the refrigerator. I warm it up and eat it with a glass of red wine.

As I eat, I pore over the small notebook Amber gave me plus her phone, on which is recorded much of her life. Her calendar. Her contacts. Her messages. Her pictures. I study every single item and commit what I can to memory.

Nothing happens all evening. No one bothers me. No one calls. Amber receives a few text messages, but they are all routine and can be ignored or answered with a few words.

At eleven that night, I've studied as much of Amber's life as I can, so I take a bath in the most luxurious tub I've ever experienced and change into a pair of white pajamas. The soft, slinky tank and pants are the most comfortable nightwear in Amber's very large collection.

I comb out my hair, the shiny blond fall hanging halfway down my back despite the trim I got this afternoon. In spite of the expensive pajamas, I still look like myself—just in strangely elegant surroundings.

I wonder if I can really fool anyone into thinking I'm

Amber.

With a sigh, I crawl into the bed, glancing over at the empty side where William must normally sleep.

A half hour after I turn off the lights, Amber's phone rings.

I've almost dozed off, so the unexpected sound causes me to sit up straight in bed, my heart racing in anxiety.

I reach over to grab the phone and see William's name and picture flashing on the screen. It's a good photo even though it's clearly a snapshot. Amber must have surprised him as he was working at his desk because he's got a wry, questioning look on his face. His hair is slightly rumpled, but he's wearing a dark suit with a loosened tie. He's got chocolate-brown eyes that convey power and intelligence.

How the hell am I going to manage to fool him?

"Hi, William," I say, keeping my voice level and casual despite the fact that the phone feels slippery in my sweaty palm.

"Did I wake you up?" he asks, sounding surprised.

"No. I was just taking it easy. How's everything going?"

There's a significant pause on the other end of the line. I gulp, afraid I've somehow already made a mistake.

But my question was completely innocuous. Surely William won't read anything suspicious in it.

I let out my breath when he replies, "I'm fine. Is this a bad time? Am I interrupting something?"

"No, of course not. I'd actually just gotten in bed. Why

would you be interrupting something?"

"No reason. You sound strange. Why did you ditch your driver this morning?"

I blink, taken aback by the sudden shift in topic and tone. "I…" I desperately search for an Amber-like answer.

"We've talked about this, Amber," William continues, sounding faintly annoyed and impatient. "And you can't keep doing it. Intentionally discarding the most basic security precautions is dangerous for both of us."

Amber must have slipped away from her driver when she arranged to meet me in the coffee shop. It was necessary today since William's driver couldn't see the two of us together. But evidently it wasn't the first time it happened.

"Amber?" he prompts. "Where did you go this morning?"

Despite my nervousness over being caught, I'm actually kind of annoyed by the man's high-handed manner. I don't have to fake my sharp tone. "I just wanted to get away for a little while. I don't like living in a fishbowl."

"You don't live in a fishbowl. You don't live in a prison. Don't be melodramatic. It's my responsibility to take care of you."

I don't answer, mostly because I'm not sure how to answer. I have no way of knowing whether William is genuinely concerned about Amber or whether he's just trying to control her. He sounds cool and professional—no emotion conveyed in his tone at all.

"Am I getting the silent treatment now?" he asks after a long pause.

"How do you expect me to react?" I'm more upset than I have any reason to feel since none of this conversation has anything to do with me personally.

"I expect you to ignore me," he replies, a slight bitterness evident in his voice. "Like you usually do."

"I don't always have to agree with you." I try for some sort of reconciliation since it doesn't seem smart to fight with William on our first conversation. "That doesn't mean I'm ignoring you. I understand why you always want me to take your car, and I'm trying to accept it. But it's hard for me to never feel... free."

William doesn't answer immediately. Then he says in a slightly milder tone, "I understand that. But I'm high profile enough to attract unwanted attention—including people who aren't mentally stable—and I don't want you to be a target because of your connection to me."

I swallow hard. The truth is, right now I'll accept any sort of security measures William wants to put into place. I'll go around with four armed bodyguards if he wants me to.

It will be a miracle to feel safe again.

All I say is, "Fine."

Another pause. "Please don't sneak away again."

"I said fine."

"Good."

"Okay. I'm kind of tired." I am tired. And I also really want to end this conversation.

"Of course. I'll talk to you tomorrow."

Thinking I've been too abrupt, I add, "Everything's all right with you?"

"Of course," William says, sounding faintly surprised again. "Everything is fine. Have a good night."

"Good night."

I hang up the phone. Then release a long groan and pull the covers up over my head.

If it's so hard to have merely a phone conversation with William, I have no idea how I'll manage to interact with him in person.

That's still a week away though. I'll be more used to being Amber by then.

I better be. Because William Worthing is a sharp, intelligent man. If Amber, with all her wiles, wasn't able to manipulate him, there's not much chance that I'll be able to do it either.

Why the hell am I even doing this? The whole thing is utterly ridiculous. Like a bad soap opera.

But then I close my eyes and let out a breath, reviewing all the locked doors and security personnel in place between me and the rest of the world.

There's no way Montaigne can reach me in here.

For tonight at least I'm safe.

2

A WEEK LATER, WILLIAM CALLS WHILE I'M EATING DINNER TO let me know he won't be home until very late tonight.

I'm ridiculously relieved since it means I can be asleep when he arrives and won't have to talk to him until morning. At this point, an extra night of safety isn't likely to make a difference, but I'll take it anyway.

The past week has gone remarkably smoothly. No one appears to suspect for even a moment that I'm not Amber.

Maybe I'm better than I thought at playing a role and putting on an act, but it can't be untapped talent alone. No one seems to know Amber at all. Like me, she's been living a life of distance, of emotional isolation. She clearly has a lot of social acquaintances—if the hundreds of contacts in her phone are any evidence—but, as she told me herself, she doesn't have any real friends.

I reply to several casual text messages a day from a

variety of affluent people who want to tell Amber about a new hairstyle, a new purchase, a new lover. But almost no one actually phones to talk to her except William, who dutifully calls once a day to check in.

A couple of days ago, I saw in Amber's calendar that she was supposed to meet a friend for lunch at a fancy bistro. I was incredibly nervous about pulling off the lunch, but it wasn't difficult at all. The friend raved about Amber's new blond hair for a while but otherwise kept up a steady, whiny ramble on her home renovations and her infuriating husband. I smiled, nodded, and made sympathetic murmurs, and that was all I needed to do to sustain the conversation.

Later that same day, William's housekeeper, Greta, made a random comment of surprise that I haven't shopped all week, evidently a significant change from Amber's normal routine, so I went shopping the next day, paying for my purchases with the credit card in Amber's wallet.

I'm sure there's a limit on the card, but the several exorbitantly priced items I bought didn't trigger it.

I didn't really want to go shopping.

Amber's huge closet is like a high-end boutique with an endless supply of luxurious silks, cashmeres, and leathers. None of the clothes fit my preferred style. All the shoes have very high heels and narrow toes. Most of the outfits are white, cream, or soft pastels—with only a few dramatic splashes of color in shoes, purses, and scarves. I've lived for the past week in constant fear of spilling something on myself and ruining an outfit worth thousands of dollars.

On my shopping trip, I was tempted to buy clothes that are more my style, but that would be a mistake. Amber obviously has a distinctive fashion sense, and any variation will draw attention to me.

So I picked out a gorgeous Prada bag in a deep purple that I absolutely love since Amber often chooses bolder colors in accessories. And then I looked for something more comfortable to sleep in.

For three nights in a row, I wore the soft white pajamas since everything else in Amber's pajama drawer is a slinky teddy or a sexy nightgown with lace and ties and other features that make it nearly impossible for me to relax in. At the store, I eyed the neatly folded piles of soft pajama pants and knit tops with visceral craving since those are exactly the kind of sleepwear I prefer. But it would be out of character for Amber, and William will be returning from his trip soon.

So I carefully picked out some other choices—decadent enough to be convincing for Amber but comfortable enough to actually sleep in. If William asks about the change of style, I'll say I'm trying something new.

After hanging up on my brief conversation with William, which mostly consisted of him telling me his flight is delayed because of bad weather, I finish my solitary dinner. Then I take a bath, put on a pair of my new pajamas—loose pants and fluttery tank made of a deep red Chinese silk—and stretch out to read in the media room, the only room in the apartment with a somewhat comfortable couch.

I've actually been rather restless this week—almost bored, if such a word can be applied with an undercurrent of lurking anxiety. I'm not sure exactly what Amber does with her time. But I can't find much to do, and I'm not long entertained by shopping or visiting day spas.

I've spent the past month cooped up in a dingy studio apartment, afraid of setting foot outside. But this week I've been freed of that fear. It's like a miracle, but it's also left me ready to do... something.

Anything.

I would love to craft some jewelry right now, but I have neither supplies nor a suitable space to work.

So I've been using the high-end exercise equipment in the workout room for hours every morning, far exceeding my maybe-once-a-week exercise routine. At least it helps get rid of some energy.

One of the only real scares I've had was yesterday when William wanted to know why I stopped going to the gym—something he must have found out from his driver since I certainly didn't mention it.

I was completely at a loss for words as I realized that,

despite the fully equipped workout room in this apartment, Amber regularly goes to a fancy health club. I knew she was a member because she gave me the information, but I've been too distracted to try to go yet.

This realization did nothing to lead me to an answer for William, who was waiting for a response to his question. Finally I managed to say, "I was just getting tired of being bothered all the time by annoying people when I try to work out."

That seemed to satisfy William, and he let the topic drop.

I keep reading on the couch until eleven when I decide I better go to bed. I need to make sure I'm "asleep" when William arrives home, which might be as early as midnight.

I'm not asleep—I'm lying in bed in the dark, nervously waiting for his arrival—at just after midnight when I hear faint sounds from the entry to the apartment.

Then the bedroom door opens.

I close my eyes immediately and lie perfectly still, deepening my breathing so my slumbers will be convincing. I hear someone walk into the room. Some rustling sounds. A drawer open and close.

Unable to stand not knowing what's going on, I peek through my lashes.

William hasn't turned on any lights, but he's left the bedroom door open, so light comes in from the hallway. I can see his dark silhouette—tall, lean, masculine—as he unbuttons his dress shirt.

His suit jacket is draped over the surface of the dresser, and he must have already taken off his tie.

I watch in genuine curiosity and growing anxiety as he takes off his cuff links and then pulls off his shirt. I can't see well enough to pick out any details of his chest, but the outline of his shoulders and the taper of his back are fit. Powerful.

I gulp, reminding myself that Amber promised there was nothing intimate between the two of them. Plus I can always have a headache. I'm not going to be required to have sex with this attractive, intimidating stranger who is about to get in bed with me.

I watch from beneath my lowered lashes as he slides off his belt, takes off his watch, and then toes off his shoes.

He's starting to unfasten his trousers when he suddenly looks over at me. I can't see his eyes or expression, but the motion of his silhouetted head is clear.

I'm so surprised by his sudden attention that I jerk a little. My heart racing frantically, I can no longer hide that I'm awake, so I lift my arms in a leisurely stretch. "Hey. You're home."

"I was trying not to wake you. You're in bed early."

He sounds mild, polite, but not particularly affectionate. Certainly not like a man who is thrilled to see Amber after a week apart.

I'm intensely relieved it's dark in the room so he won't able to see me very clearly. "Yeah. I was tired. How was your trip?"

He pauses, still focused on where I'm lying in bed. I momentarily lose my breath, as it feels like his scrutiny might pierce through the dark of the room. But that's ridiculous. I simply need to stay relaxed and act natural.

"Fine," he replies at last, taking off his trousers. He seems to be wearing some kind of dark-colored boxers beneath them, but I can't clearly see the cut or fabric.

"Good." After the groggy response, I snuggle down under the covers as if I'm about to drift back to sleep. I don't feel tired at all. I'm having trouble controlling my shallow breathing and racing heartbeat. But I don't want William to get any ideas about nighttime activities, so it's best if he thinks I'm not fully awake.

At the sound of more motion, I peek out again and see that he has gathered his clothes and is heading into the closet. After a minute in there, he goes into the bathroom and closes the door behind him.

I let out a long breath. It's fine. I can do this. William and Amber might sleep in the same bed, but they're clearly quite distant, exactly as Amber explained. I can act even more distant. William might think I'm rude and heartless, but at least he'll still think I'm Amber.

I hear the toilet flush in the bathroom. Then the water running in the sink. He's probably brushing his teeth. I wonder if he'll take a shower, but he doesn't. He comes back out after just a minute, turning off the bathroom light and then closing the bedroom door.

The room falls into almost complete darkness, broken only by the thin edge of light around the door and the faint glow of the bedside clock.

I hear rather than see William walk over and climb into the bed beside me. The mattress shifts. The covers are adjusted. My pillow moves slightly, nudged by his.

I feel him stretch out beside me. Hear him let out a deep, thick breath— as if he's trying to relax.

He must be tired. He flew in from London. He's likely had a long, hard week.

And he hasn't had a very warm homecoming.

I feel a sharp pang in my chest. It's not guilt—since William obviously isn't my responsibility—but it's something like sympathy. He's been basically nice to me every time we've talked on the phone. Not sentimental or emotional but certainly not rude, abrasive, or cold.

He's been away from his fiancée for more than a week, and he's been greeted as if I couldn't care less that he's home.

It doesn't matter if it's more a business arrangement than a real relationship. If I was in his place, I might be hurt.

I'm not used to spending much time worrying about other people's feelings, not since I left home. And lately

I've had no emotional bandwidth for anything but dealing with Montaigne.

But right now I'm supposed to be Amber. And Amber and William live in the same home and share a bed.

So I roll over onto my side so I'm facing in William's direction. My eyes have adjusted, and I can see the outline of his head against the pillow, the lines of his lean body under the covers. "So your trip was all right?" I make sure to still sound a little sleepy.

He pauses and turns his head to look in my direction. "Yes. It was fine."

I search my mind for something to ask that doesn't require any real knowledge of the purpose of his trip—which I have no idea about.

"Nothing exciting happened?"

"No. Just normal meetings."

He doesn't seem very talkative, which is actually a relief. If he doesn't want to share, then I'm not obliged to act like a supportive partner. "Okay." Acting on instinct, I lean toward him. Amber told me they kiss sometimes, and surely this is an appropriate situation for a brief peck. "I'm glad you're home."

I can see well enough in the dark to find his lips. I press a soft kiss there, prepared to draw back almost imme-diately.

William's mouth is perfectly still at first—as if he isn't sure how to respond. But then his lips soften and cling to mine unexpectedly, and he raises a hand to my hair to hold my head in place before I can withdraw.

He's a good kisser—that much is clear—and I feel a completely unexpected flutter of pleasure as our lips move together and his tongue flicks out to tease mine lightly.

But then the pleasure is swallowed up by a much deeper swell of panic.

I don't know this man.

I don't *know* him.

And he thinks he's kissing Amber.

So I pull away, making myself smile in a relaxed manner. "Good night, William." I roll over onto my opposite side and snuggle down under the covers again.

"Good night."

I can feel his eyes on me in the dark for a minute. Then he rolls over too, his back toward me, and after a few minutes, his breathing slows and deepens into sleep.

It takes a long time before I can fall asleep too.

Something wakes me the next morning, but I'm not sure what it is.

I shift in bed, enjoying the feel of silk and Egyptian cotton against my skin. Then I stretch and manage to open my eyes, feeling leisurely and comfortable.

I suck in a sharp breath as I abruptly realize where I am, who I am, and who I'm with.

It's just after six in the morning, and William is standing in front of the dresser in the bedroom, fastening the cuff links on his french-blue dress shirt. He must have already showered since he's almost fully dressed in black trousers, shoes, and socks.

He glances over, sees I'm awake. "Morning."

"Morning," I mumble back, trying to wake up. It would be a big mistake to try to carry on a conversation with William without being fully in possession of my faculties. I sit up in bed since the change in position might help my mind to work more quickly.

He's finished with his cuff links and is now working on his tie, but he's staring at me with such obvious attention that I almost cringe.

"What?" I finally demand when he does nothing but stare. My red silk pajamas are generally flattering, although I don't like how my nipples are poking out through the fabric and how one of the straps keeps slipping down over my shoulder. My hair is almost certainly messy, but I just woke up. Surely Amber doesn't look perfect first thing every morning either.

"Why did you change your hair?" he asks at last.

I almost gasp in relief as I realize why he's been so absorbed in my appearance. I forgot that he hasn't seen Amber's new blond hair.

Masking my expression, I give a little shrug. "I just felt like a change. Don't you like it?"

His brown eyes scrutinize every detail of my appearance. His gaze is mostly focused on my hair, but I notice it also slips down to linger briefly on my breasts.

He and Amber are engaged to be married. Of course he's allowed to look. But it still makes me feel strangely naked, exposed.

"You don't like it?" I ask when he doesn't answer. Any woman in the world would feel insecure if she thought the man in her life didn't like her new hairdo, so I know the slight quaver in my voice is exactly right.

"Of course I like it." He's still studying me with frightening scrutiny. He tightens his tie and reaches over for his suit jacket. "It just takes some getting used to. It makes you look really different."

I suddenly realize what a great advantage the apparent change in hair color is. A major alteration of appearance like that can also explain any other slight incongruities William might notice. Hair can make eye color, facial shape, and skin tone seem different too. Surely a dramatic change from brunette to blond will mask the very minor differences between my appearance and Amber's.

"Well, I like it," I say, patting my messy hair. I'm starting to feel too self-conscious under his observant eyes, so I climb out of bed, mumbling that I need some coffee.

I'm able to escape for long enough to get a cup of

coffee, and when I return, William is sitting on the edge of the bed and reading a message on his phone.

"Everything all right?" I ask when I see his eyebrows draw together, creating little lines of worry on his forehead.

He glances up, as if he's surprised. "Of course."

There isn't any "of course" about it. He's clearly distracted by whatever message he received, and it has obviously concerned him. His shoulders look a little tense, and his jaw is set tightly.

"What is it?" As far as I can tell on our brief acquaintance, he seems like a basically decent guy. I don't like this change in his demeanor. It means something is wrong with him. I sit on the bed beside him, holding my coffee mug in both hands. "Did something happen?"

His eyes cut over to my face, and for a moment he looks like he's going to say something, like he's going to share whatever is bothering him. But then he gives an almost imperceptible shake of his head. "It's nothing, Amber. Nothing for you to worry about."

My mouth tightens in annoyance. He's clearly hiding things from me, shutting me out. My first instinct is to resist such treatment. I want to know what's wrong.

But I stifle the irrational instinct. Obviously, William and Amber have their regular habits—which seem to consist of holding each other at arm's length. I would be incredibly foolish if I don't take advantage of this situation.

The more distanced I am from William, the safer I'll be.

"Okay. Good." I sip my coffee.

He shoots me a strange look I can't interpret and then gets up, buttoning his suit jacket as he does. "I've got to get to the office. I have a dinner meeting, so I'll be back late tonight."

If I was really his fiancée, I'd definitely have something to say about his working all day after being gone for a week. But, as it is, his absence adds to my advantage. "Okay. Have a good day."

He stands looking at me for a minute, as if he's waiting for something.

Hit with a sudden realization, I stand up too. I stretch up to kiss him on the mouth, carefully holding my coffee away so I don't spill it on his lovely suit. He smells delicious—warm, masculine, faintly expensive, nothing too obvious or obnoxious.

He kisses me back, gently stroking the length of my hair as he pulls away. His brow is lowered when he looks down at me again.

I freeze, wondering if he can tell the difference between my kisses and Amber's. Obviously, people have their own ways of kissing. But how different could such a simple kiss be?

"I'll talk to you later." Then he walks out of the room.

I release a rough sigh and flop back down on the bed, relieved to be alone again.

So far, things have gone all right. But this is going to get really complicated fast.

William doesn't get home until after eight that evening. And then, after grabbing a sandwich from the kitchen and giving me a brief greeting, he disappears into the one locked room in the apartment—which is obviously his home office.

Despite myself, I'm a little offended.

This is how he treats Amber? He's gone for days and then all she gets of his time is a brief conversation on his way out the door that morning? He finally comes home, only to hide himself away in his office. What the hell kind of situation is this?

One tiny, irrational part of me is tempted to storm his office and demand he treat me like I'm more than an expensive accessory in his life.

I don't, of course. The more he works, the less time he'll have to recognize that I'm not really Amber. The less I'll have to deal with the panic always simmering beneath the surface as I think and rethink every word I say to him.

I take a long, hot bubble bath, which I've been doing every evening since the tub is so luxurious and it helps relax me before bed. Then I put on another new set of pajamas I bought the other day—a soft, white lace camisole and silk knit pants in a deep blue. Since it's a little cool in the room, I add a white belted sweater before I go into the media room.

Instead of reading, I turn on the television, which is set to a channel playing a British comedy. At first I'm just curious, so I pause before switching to a streaming network. But then I start to snicker over the dry, clever humor.

An hour later, I'm still laughing, completely wrapped up with the show and momentarily forgetting I'm supposed to be Amber.

I'm by myself, stretched out on the cushy leather sofa with a glass of white wine in my hand and a soft throw tossed over my legs. And I can't seem to stop laughing.

I break off abruptly when I realize that William is standing in the doorway. He's taken off his suit jacket and loosened his tie, but otherwise he's wearing what he put on that morning. His eyes are startlingly dark above the french blue of his shirt. They're fixed on my face.

I have no way of interpreting his expression. But I'm nervous and self-conscious as I straighten up on the couch where I've been stretched out in a careless sprawl. "Hey. You done working?"

He makes a brief gesture with his hand, almost as if he's brushing away my question. His eyes bore into me and then shift to the television screen.

"It's silly—I know." I have to fight not to babble nervously at his expression. "But it's kind of funny."

Maybe William is surprised since Amber might not have been in the habit of chortling uninhibitedly over British comedy. But my sister used to have a similar sense of humor. As girls, we would giggle for hours over exactly the same things.

Surely something so trivial won't be an obvious giveaway.

William's eyes have returned to my face. Then they lower to the wineglass in my hand. Something changes on his expression. It tightens or darkens or something.

I have no idea what's happening, so I blink when he turns on his heel and strides back down the hallway, away from me.

I stand up automatically. He's angry about something. And I have no idea what it is.

Not knowing what else to do, I follow him. Find him in the entry hall, rifling through my new purple Prada bag.

"What the hell are you doing?" I'm immediately angry at the violation—even though almost nothing in the bag is mine. I'm also washed with a cold wave of panic, remembering the little notebook with all of Amber's information is in there.

William completely ignores me. He pulls out Amber's shiny, engraved, silver pillbox, and I now know what he's looking for.

Several days ago, as I was searching for an aspirin in Amber's bag, I found in that container a large collection of pills that were definitely not aspirin.

They looked like prescription medication. Some were white and round. Some were small and blue. And there were a couple of oblong yellowish ones.

Maybe prescription pills are one of Amber's vices. I'm not going to have anything to do with it. I flushed the mysterious pills and filled the little compartment with ibuprofen instead.

When he flips the lid up, William blinks down at the harmless over-the-counter pills, obviously taken aback by not finding what he expects.

"Satisfied?" I snap, still deeply annoyed by him searching my purse without permission. "I can't tell you how much trouble I get into with my little hoard of Advil!"

He stares up at me. "Where are they?"

"Where are what?" I don't need to fake my indignation. My spine stiffens, and my cheeks flush with rising emotion.

"Where are the pills? I'm not a fool, Amber. I knew you were acting strange. I told you I wasn't going to let you—"

"There are no pills. And I don't give a fuck what you'll let me do. Who the hell do you think you are?" It's been a long time since I lost my temper. Most of the time I just don't care enough to bother anymore. I have no idea why

I'm so upset now—since all this is about Amber and not me.

William takes one long step over and grabs my upper arms. He looks cold and hard rather than fiery, and his hands on my arms are strong but don't hurt. "I have every right to know this. We came to an agreement, and if you're using again, then you've broken your side of it."

My mind is a whirl. I have no idea what's going on here, and my ignorance is frightening since I might not know enough to sustain my stolen identity.

"I'm not on any pills." I don't like the feel of his hands on my arms. They're not violent. They're intimate. "I haven't broken our agreement."

Amber had definitely broken it. She'd had those pills —maybe she'd been addicted to them. And she'd certainly betrayed William in other ways.

For just a moment, I'm hotly angry with Amber for acting the way she is.

William stares at me, his eyes so penetrating I feel utterly naked.

"You don't believe me," I say when he doesn't respond.

"No. I don't."

"Then search my purse." I thrust the bag over at him almost violently. I desperately hope he won't do it since that notebook is definitely in there. But it's better than him looking like I betrayed him. "Search the room. Search the whole damned place. There's nothing here to find."

I immediately regret the angry declaration since I have no way of knowing whether Amber stashed her stuff around the apartment in hidden corners.

But all the intensity leaves William anyway. He doesn't take the purse I thrust at him, and his hands drop from my arms.

He stares, and for just a moment he looks bewildered, almost vulnerable.

William Worthing isn't a vulnerable man.

The flicker of helplessness I see on his face makes something clench hard in my chest. I'm doing this because I'm desperate, because I don't see any other good option.

But it isn't fair to William.

This is his life I'm manipulating.

Absurdly, I want to comfort him, but there's absolutely nothing I can do. I let out a thick sigh and finally land on a way out of this trap of an encounter.

"I've... I've been doing a lot of thinking." I don't have to feign the self-consciousness and hesitations. "I know I've messed up a lot. I'm trying... I'm trying to be better."

His eyes narrow as he watches me. He doesn't say anything.

"I'm... trying." I lower my lashes to hide my eyes. "Maybe that's why you think I seem... I seem different."

When several moments pass and he doesn't say anything—all I can hear is his heavy breathing—I peek up at him. His face has softened slightly, and his eyes aren't so hard on my face.

I let out a relieved breath, hoping I've managed to protect my identity and smooth over the conflict with one stroke. "Okay?"

He inclines his head and lets out his breath. "Okay."

I swallow hard. Then lean over to pick up my bag. I replace the pillbox and the small mirror that slipped out in William's search.

I return the purse to its place in the entry hall and walk back to the media room since there's nothing else for me to do.

William doesn't join me again. He must go back into his office. At midnight, I head to bed.

An hour later, William comes to bed too.

I'm no longer used to intimacy of any kind, but that's how it feels when William climbs under the covers beside me. I have to remind myself it's all a pretense. This is Amber's life, not mine. William is Amber's fiancé, not mine.

Eventually, either Amber will come back to claim her life again or it will be safe enough for me to reclaim mine.

It will only complicate matters if I start to feel sympathy or annoyance or any real emotion at all with William.

I only need to maintain the illusion.

The illusion is all that matters. And it's extraordinarily

delicate, like a mirror that will shatter with too much pressure.

I pretend to sleep, but I can smell William in bed beside me. His scent is different than it was this morning—still faintly expensive but not as crisp. He smells more natural now. Like a real man.

The bed shifts as he adjusts positions. I can feel him looking at me silently in the dark.

This time I don't open my eyes.

3

THE NEXT FEW DAYS PASS WITHOUT ANY FURTHER DRAMA.

William gets up early every morning and heads to the office, usually before I get out of bed. He doesn't return until close to seven in the evenings. He gets his own dinner —something quick and easy—and takes it to eat in his home office, where he only emerges to exercise in the workout room for a while, then showers and goes to bed.

He will occasionally ask a question that momentarily stumps me—like the other day when he wanted to know what I did with a pair of his cuff links—but I've managed to muddle through those moments well enough, often by pleading ignorance, as I had with the cuff links.

Holding on to the pretense of being Amber is easy because I hardly interact with him at all. The confrontation when he was searching for pills is the longest conversation we've ever had.

I should be relieved. I am. Of course.

But I'm also faintly annoyed with him.

The man needs to do something other than work. What the hell is he even thinking? How is sitting at a desk or in conference rooms every minute of the day good for someone? He's going to work himself into a heart attack— not to mention carpal tunnel and migraines and lower back problems and high blood pressure and whatever other health issues come from constant work.

Plus he basically ignores my existence. It's convenient for me, but he doesn't know that. Maybe I actually want him to spend time with the woman he lives with and is going to marry.

Amber said he's controlling. Other than his indignation over the pills and his confronting me about Amber ditching her driver, I haven't noticed anything remotely controlling about him. Maybe the pills were the main issue she had with him.

I can hardly blame him for not wanting those pills in his home.

She also said he's bossy, and I can maybe see that in the somewhat blunt, professional manner he deals with things. He probably hasn't had a lot of experience being in intimate relationships. After all, he clearly has nothing in his life except work.

His manner doesn't bother me, but his absence does. Even though I know it shouldn't.

On Friday afternoon, he calls around five and tells me he's working late and won't be home until ten or eleven.

I bite back my instinctive objection and tell him sweetly that's fine and thanks for letting me know.

I'm scowling as I disconnect the call.

The man needs a good, firm shake. Is he going to work every hour of the weekend too?

Purposefully I blow out the annoyance and clear my mind. Other than William's aggravating workaholic tendencies, this second week has gone fine. No one is remotely suspicious of my identity. I've had very few tense encounters. And I've almost stopped looking over my shoulder and scanning every newcomer when I'm out.

I can actually sleep at night and relax when I'm alone in the apartment. It seems like forever since I've felt this way.

If for no other reason, taking Amber's place is worth it simply for the reprieve it's given me from constant fear of Montaigne.

I eat dinner by myself—ordering in from an Italian place a few blocks away—and leave the leftovers in the refrigerator in case William wants them when he finally gets home. I've started doing that when I have extra from my dinner, leaving a note on the container that says he's welcome to them if he wants.

Every morning any leftovers I leave in the refrigerator are gone.

Bored and restless and irrationally lonely, I wander the beautifully furnished rooms. Try to watch some television. Try to read a book. Then finally give up and decide to go ahead and take a bath and then go to bed early.

I have got to figure out something to do to fill my time since I'm not living in heightened anxiety every minute anymore.

I run a bath in the big soaking tub and add some fancy honey-and-lavender bath oil that creates a light foam of pleasant bubbles. I turn on the sound system and leave it on the classical music it's set to. Then I clip up my hair and drop my clothes on the floor of the bathroom before I climb into the tub.

I stretch out, submerged in the deliciously scented hot water. Close my eyes and try to relax.

I wonder when William will get home. Probably not for another two hours.

I wonder if he has a woman on the side. My blood pressure rises at the thought alone. He's in his midthirties. He likely still has a sex drive.

But when would he even have time for an affair? He's at work all the time.

Maybe he's screwing his assistant. Turning her over the desk and fucking her with his suit on.

I have to blow out slow breaths until the random image leaves my mind.

There's no reason to assume any such thing. And even if it were true, it wouldn't have anything to do with me.

I'm not the one under contract to marry him.

He wouldn't be betraying me.

I just don't like the idea of him betraying anyone.

I've almost succeeded at clearing my mind when the bathroom door—which I closed, as I always do when I take a bath—suddenly swings open.

William stands in the doorway, one hand on his tie like he was in the process of loosening it before he froze. He's staring at me, as surprised and dumbfounded as I am.

"Hey!" I manage to say, pushing over more bubbles on the top of the water to make sure my body is suitably masked.

"Sorry." He blinks. Stares some more. Then blinks again. "Sorry. I thought you were out."

"Why would I be out?"

He frowns. "Because it's Friday. You're always out on Friday evenings."

I didn't know this about Amber. Maybe I should have. "If you didn't expect me to be here, then why did you call to tell me you're working late?"

"Seemed like the decent thing to do." He's finally managed to pull his tie looser, although he doesn't pull it off altogether. I see his eyes dip down to the water and then back to my face.

The quick look gets me kind of excited, which is absolutely ridiculous. "Oh."

"I'll leave you al—"

"It's fine," I say with a sigh. "You can come in. It's your bathroom, after all." The toilet is enclosed with a door, so if he needs to use that, he can still do so in privacy.

He hesitates briefly before coming in. He apparently doesn't need to use the bathroom. He shrugs out of his suit jacket and then splashes a lot of water on his face.

"What time is it?" I ask when he picks up a hand towel to dry his face and neck. "I thought you were working until ten or eleven."

"It's almost nine thirty. We finished up earlier than I thought."

Again, I'm hit with the image of him fucking a faceless woman over the desk.

"What's the matter?" he asks, leaning against the long vanity countertop.

"What do you mean?"

"It looked like something's bothering you."

Damn. I've got to get control of my thoughts better than this. I'm going to blow all the work I've put into this ridiculous scheme.

"Oh no. It's nothing. I just had an itch." It's the first excuse that crosses my mind.

He pauses like he's waiting.

"What?" I prompt.

"Aren't you going to scratch it?"

"Oh. Yeah." Feeling like a fool, I lift my foot out of the water and bend my knee until I can reach my ankle, scratching the wet skin for a minute even though it wasn't remotely itchy.

He's watching me the whole time, his head cocked, his mouth tilted up very slightly in a glimmer of a bemused smile.

"You shouldn't laugh at me," I tell him as I sink my leg and foot back into the water.

"Was I laughing?"

"It looked like you secretly were."

His mouth twitches up for real. Brief but unmistakable.

I feel like smiling too, but instead, I put on Amber's pout. "You're doing it again."

"Maybe I am."

Okay. This has to stop. I'm about to melt into goo for absolutely no reason. I'm simply not the gooey type, and there's no way I can let down my guard. So I clear my throat and say, "Can you do me a big favor?"

"Sure." He puts the hand towel down next to the sink.

"Can you get me a glass of wine? I think there's half a bottle of white in the refrigerator. I'm not ready to get out of the tub yet."

"Of course." He looks surprised but not annoyed or impatient. He doesn't appear to think I'm asking for anything unreasonable.

I don't actually need a glass of wine. I just need a break from him for a minute.

I use it to remind myself of who I am and what I'm doing here, so the warmth in my chest has been properly contained when William returns to the bathroom.

He's got two glasses of wine in his hands. He hands me one and then sits on the bench against the wall next to the tub and takes a sip of the other glass.

So kill me. I get a little thrill that he's stayed.

"You look tired," I tell him since one of us needs to say something.

He does look tired. Exhausted. His white shirt is wrinkled and slightly damp in the middle of the back. There are shadows under his eyes, and he needs to shave, although I'm sure he shaved this morning.

His hair is way too long. It's styled in what's clearly supposed to be a short cut, but he's gone too long between trims. He's got a lot of it—a warm, medium brown with only a few threads of gray sprinkled in—and it doesn't lie neatly. It kinks up in odd places.

I like it. I really want to reach over and smooth it down.

"I am tired," he says, slightly hoarse.

"Well, that's your own fault. You work at least fifteen hours every day. It's not good for you."

He makes a faint huff, his eyes slanting over toward me in discreet scrutiny.

"I'm serious. You're never going to not be tired unless

you cut back a little and get some real rest and maybe even do something for fun."

"I can't cut back right now. Too much going on."

"What's going on?" I'm filled with that annoyed impatience over his work schedule again. When I suddenly remember this might be something I'm already supposed to know, I add, "I mean, is it anything new?"

He doesn't appear to find anything strange about the question. "We're doing a lot of reorganization of the Worthing holdings. It's a ton of work."

"Oh." I frown. "What kind of reorganization?"

"Arthur—my cousin, you met him once, do you remember? He's changing the structure so he's not the final authority on everything."

"I see." This must be new information to Amber as well as to me, so surely I'm allowed to ask more questions. "Why is he doing that?"

"It's always been set up in a ridiculous archaic way. Where the oldest male heir has to sign off on everything."

My mouth drops open slightly. "So you haven't been the final decision-maker on the companies you run?"

His shoulders shake slightly, like he's silently laughing. Dry and sardonic. "No, I have not. As I said, it's ridiculous. A remnant of patriarchal assholes in my family tree. But Arthur's changing it, which is a good thing. But it's a lot of work to reorganize in a way to make my companies separate and self-sufficient from the rest of the Worthing assets."

"It sounds like it will be worth it in the end if you actually will get to make your own decisions."

"Yeah. I think so."

There's a flicker of something on his face. Maybe reluctance. Maybe anxiety. "What's the matter? Aren't you excited about it?"

"Sure. It's what I've wanted for a long time. But... it's a big weight on me. A lot of expectation."

Amber told me that William was desperate for the approval of his family, so much so that he entered into the agreement with Amber to get the Delacourte brand and name. I ask softly, "Who are you afraid of disappointing?"

He stares at an empty spot in the air for a long time. Then shifts his eyes to meet mine. "Everyone?"

I make a weird little whimper and reach over to put a wet hand on his knee. I don't have any idea what to say.

Searching my mind for what I researched on the Worthing family, I remember that William's father is dead. So is at least one of his uncles. "I didn't get a good sense of Arthur when I met him. Is he not a decent guy?"

"No, he is a good guy. Brilliant. And he never cared all that much about business. He was doing the job because he was born into it and he thought he had to."

"So he should be relieved to pass off most of the responsibility. He's not going to be disappointed in you.

Who else are you worried about?" I've completely forgotten about my role as Amber. I really want to know the answer.

William doesn't answer immediately. He's staring in my direction but not really seeing me. Finally he murmurs thickly, "Sometimes it feels like there are generations of Worthings all lined up to judge me."

My chest aches at the deep feeling in the brief comment. "But they're dead."

"Even so."

"Was your...?" I clear my throat. "Was your father... like that?"

"Oh yes." He shifts slightly, meeting my gaze for real. "He was like that. Every Worthing in the older generations was like that."

"But Arthur isn't. What about your other cousins? You have a bunch of them, don't you?" I'm purposefully vague since I'm not sure how much of this information I'm already supposed to know.

Evidently not much. He clearly never shared much of a personal nature with Amber. "Yeah. Most of them are okay. I'm not sure how we turned out okay, to be honest."

"That's good then. So it will be fine. You'll work hard, but you'll do a good job. And no one will be disappointed in you. They'll see how great you are."

He swallows so hard I can see it in his throat. He

glances away but then back to me in a quick look, like he's checking to make sure I'm being serious.

I am. Dead serious. My eyes are wide, and my lips are wobbling slightly since I'm far more emotional than is entirely appropriate.

His mouth softens. "Thanks."

My cheeks flush hot. I hide behind a long sip of wine.

We sit in silence for a couple of minutes, but it doesn't feel awkward. We're just lost in our own thoughts.

Then he asks, "So why didn't you go out tonight?"

I shrug. "I just didn't feel like it."

"Are you going to go out tomorrow?"

"Probably not." I might as well tell him the truth. Even if I knew exactly what Amber does when she goes out, there's not much chance I'm going to be up to doing it too, even if it's the best way to maintain my cover.

"I see." It looks like he's thinking, processing.

"What?" I prompt.

"Nothing. I was just wondering if you might change your mind about tomorrow."

I freeze, completely confused. Disoriented. I have no idea what he's talking about.

"You can still come to the garden party at the Harrows with me. If you want. No worries either way." He sounds like he's being intentionally casual.

"Oh. Okay. Well. Yeah. I guess I can do that."

His expression changes. He doesn't smile, but there's

something surprised and pleased in his eyes that makes me really happy I said yes. "Great."

"Can you... can you remind me of the details?"

"Sure." He pulls out his phone and appears to forward me something. "I know you don't like Mimi Harrow, but I'm sure you can manage to avoid her most of the time."

That's a helpful piece of information for me. What else am I going to need to know?

What have I gotten myself into?

"Yeah. I'll do my best."

"Do you plan to tell me what that was all about?" William asks the following day, looking at me with cool, rather distant brown eyes.

We're both seated in the back of his car, and I haven't said much in the seven minutes since we left the Harrows' huge estate about forty miles outside DC.

My feet are hurting from standing around in four-inch heels for three hours. My face is sore from the polite smile I held on my face during the entire length of the garden party. And I had one glass of champagne too many, so my head is spinning just a little.

I really don't feel up to dealing with an interrogation—especially without any warning or preparation.

I thought things were better between us after our conversation last night.

I frown, just as cool as William is. "What do you mean?"

He arches his eyebrows in a slightly impatient expression. "You've never behaved that way at a social function before. So either something is going on you're not telling me or a stranger has taken possession of your body."

I gulp, my heart starting to race as a surge of panic rises fast.

Is this it? Have I finally been found out after thirteen days as Amber?

"That's ridiculous," I say, mostly to give myself more time to wrap my mind around what William is referring to. "I'm not up to anything."

"Then why were you acting that way?"

I still have no idea what he's talking about. I thought the garden party this afternoon went pretty well. I was really nervous since it was the first big social function I've attended with William, and I was surrounded by dozens of people who know Amber and might recognize that I'm not her.

I was even nervous about what to wear since my previous social experiences have never included fancy garden parties at sprawling estates. I puttered about with my hair and makeup until William finished getting dressed so I could take my cue from him. When he emerged from the closet in an elegant beige suit with a slightly darker tan tie, I realized I should wear a dress instead of the stylish pants I'd been considering.

I found a cream-colored dress in Amber's closet and paired it with a chocolate-brown scarf and heels. And I was vastly relieved when I arrived at the party and saw from the clothes of the other women that I'd chosen my wardrobe exactly right.

The party wasn't particularly painful. The formal gardens and old-fashioned setting were lovely and romantic, and everyone I talked to was civil and pleasant with the exception of one gorgeous brunette who clearly had a thing for William. I acted as if that woman didn't exist while making sure to block her access to him. Otherwise, I let him do most of the talking and just stayed at his side, smiling, laughing, and murmuring agreement in appropriate places.

I don't have a clue about how Amber would have acted differently at a social function.

When I only stare, William goes on, "Amber? I'm serious. I want to know what's going on. You might have agreed to go to social functions, but you've always made it clear you'd rather not be there. Why are you suddenly acting like the perfect partner today?" He sounds faintly annoyed, as if his inability to figure me out is a source of frustration to him.

My lips part slightly as I try to hide my utter astonishment. I've gotten a clear sense that the details of William's relationship with Amber were ironed out through negotiation and a contract, but I still haven't been able to figure out all the nuances.

Even given the practical nature of their relationship, surely he wasn't happy with a fiancée who was so uncooperative. Surely the Delacourte name isn't so important to him that he'll put up with downright bad behavior.

The thought bothers me more than it should. Not that I have a problem with William prioritizing whatever he wants, but he seems better than that somehow—like he deserves more.

I clear my throat, stalling a moment longer as I come up with a response. "I... I told you before that I'm trying to do better."

William peers at me so intently that I almost squirm.

"Don't you...?" My cheeks warm with an emotion I can't quite identify. "Don't you like it?"

"I do like it." His voice is strangely thick. His eyes never leave my face. "I just don't believe it."

I look away from him, out the window of the car, momentarily afraid that I'll collapse into a pitiful heap and admit everything to him. He must be on the verge of figuring it out anyway.

But he doesn't know everything. He can't know. He knows something is different, but surely it would never occur to him that another person has somehow taken over his fiancée's identity. Amber told me he never knew about me—that she has an identical twin sister. She and our dad cut me out of their lives completely after I left and pretended I never existed. So William would consider every other possibility before he would believe that I've actually taken Amber's place.

He almost certainly thinks I'm up to something, that I'm trying to manipulate him.

And he isn't wrong about that.

When my anxiety and confusion fade slightly, I'm flooded by an unexpected wave of sympathy. For William.

He's not a bad guy overall. He comes off as cold, calculating, and guarded—and he is all those things to a certain extent. But even in the brief interactions I've had with him so far, I can tell that he's also sensitive. And surprisingly vulnerable. For whatever reasons, he is committed to Amber, and she's clearly taken advantage of that commitment.

And now I'm lying to William, using him, manipulating him.

My motivations might be different, but my actions aren't any better than Amber's.

But things have gone too far, and I'm not sure what other choices I have. I want to stay safe and make a gesture in support of my sister. This is the only means I have of doing both.

I jump when I feel a hand on my upper arm. I jerk my

head back to see that William has reached over to touch me gently. "Amber?" His voice is softer than it was before. "If something is going on with you, if you're in some sort of trouble, if something is wrong, you need to tell me what it is. How can I help if I don't know what it is?"

I take a deep breath. Shake my head. "I'm fine. It's just what I told you before. I feel bad about... about how I've acted. So I'm trying to do better."

He doesn't answer. And I don't know if he believes me or not.

4

――――――

THE NEXT WEEK, WE GO BACK TO NORMAL WITH WILLIAM working all the time and me doing whatever I can think of to do as Amber.

It's a safe week but not a particularly good one. It feels like I'm simply waiting around the whole time.

For what, I have no idea.

On the following Saturday morning, I wake up knowing it's early and the weekend. My schedule as Amber allows me to sleep in on any day I want, but weekends feel different anyway.

I reposition myself, rolling over onto my side, and snuggle under the thick, soft duvet.

A soft sound—halfway between a grunt and a sigh—from the other side of the bed makes me pop my eyes open. William.

I've never woken up in the morning with him still in bed.

He's definitely still here, sleeping on his back with one arm out from under the covers. His eyes are closed. His chest rises and falls with slow, even breathing. His jaw is dark with a day's worth of stubble. The coarse hair on his arm is slightly ruffled.

I really like the sight of him right now. Relaxed. Soft. Vulnerable. It does something weird to my chest. And I swear also to my ovaries.

I'm giving myself an internal lecture about how I need to stop being stupid and either roll back over or get up when William moves slightly. His hand grips the duvet, and his head shifts on the pillow. Before I can react, he blinks a few times and opens his eyes, peering at me from between his dark lashes.

"Hi," I say rather foolishly.

"Hi." He blinks again. Clears his throat. "Did I sleep in?"

"Not really. I just woke up early for some reason."

"Ah." He reaches up to add a second pillow behind his head, lifting his position slightly. "How long have you been awake?"

"Just a couple of minutes."

"Have you been lying there looking at me?" He slants me a curious look, but he appears more intrigued than annoyed.

"No. Of course not."

He picks his phone up from the nightstand, glancing at the screen before putting it back down. There appears to be a collection of notifications there, but he ignores them. He was probably just checking the time.

It's 5:23.

"You should stay in bed a little longer," I tell him.

"Why?"

"Because it's not even six on a Saturday morning. Why do you have to get up?"

"I don't."

"Good."

"I didn't say I wasn't going to get up. Just that I don't have to."

I frown at him. "Are you seriously going to get up and start working at five thirty on a weekend morning?"

He checks my expression. Then relaxes back against the pillow. "I don't know. I'm not much for lying around doing nothing."

"Yeah. I know the feeling." I've had three weeks of doing nothing, and it's really getting old. "But still. You do need some rest."

"I guess."

"There's no guess about it. It's an absolute definite."

His mouth twitches up slightly. "Okay."

"Okay it's a definite? Or okay you'll take it easy this morning?"

"I'm not sure how easy I'll take it all morning, but I won't get up right now."

"Oh. Then that's good." My cheeks are warm for no good reason. I feel myself smiling at him.

His face softens even more. "Yes. Good."

I do my best not to giggle as I pull the covers up farther over my shoulders. I close my eyes since we're supposed to be resting. But after a few minutes, I have to peek between my slitted eyes to see if William is watching me.

He is.

His head is turned slightly in my direction, and his eyes are quietly observant on my face. He doesn't look suspicious or affectionate or annoyed or amused.

He looks faintly bewildered, and it goes straight to my heart.

Of course he's bewildered. He knows something is off, but he can't figure out what it is.

Shaking off the soft emotions, I manage to keep my tone light. "You're staring at me."

"And?"

"And it's disturbing my slumbers."

"You weren't asleep."

"I was working on it. And I could feel your eyes boring into me."

"That sounds painful."

"It was. How would you like to have eyes boring into you at five thirty in the morning?"

He chuckles. "I woke up to you staring at me."

"I wasn't staring!"

"Weren't you?"

"No. I just haven't..." I catch myself before saying I haven't really seen him sleep before because I have no way of knowing if that's true of Amber. "I'm just used to you getting up at the crack of dawn."

"Yeah." He lets out a long, thick sigh. Almost a groan.

The textured exhale does dangerous things to my insides.

"I guess I am kind of tired," he admits, closing his eyes.

His eyelashes aren't unusually long, but they're thick and dark and look striking against the shadowed skin under his eyes.

"Of course you're tired. No one can work as much as you and not be tired. Why don't you take the weekend off?"

"I can't. I've got a conference call at eleven this morning."

I sneer. What the hell kind of ridiculous people set up a business call on a Saturday? "Okay. Fine. Then take tomorrow off. Surely you don't have anything on your schedule for a Sunday."

"No. I don't."

"Okay then. It's settled. You're taking tomorrow off."

His shoulders shake a few times in silent laughter. "Shouldn't I have a say in settling such a thing?"

"No. Not really. You've shown yourself to be completely

incompetent at managing a reasonable work schedule, so I'm having to make an executive decision." I pause. It feels like he's responding well to my teasing bossiness, but that doesn't mean he's going to agree. So my voice is softer, more hesitant, as I add, "So will you take tomorrow off?"

"I guess I have to if you've made an executive decision about it." He's smiling, fond and still amused.

I gulp at the look.

It's Amber's expression.

It's not mine.

He must see something on my face because his smile fades. "What's the matter?"

"Nothing." I beam at him to prove it.

He's not convinced. "Why have you been doing this?"

"Doing what?"

"I don't know. Being real. Enjoying yourself. Then it's like something goes through your mind that takes it away from you. And you get sad again."

Shit, he's good. Way too observant. Way too smart. He's put a lot of very slim clues together in exactly the right way. The only thing he's missing is that Amber has a twin.

"I'm not sad."

"I don't believe you."

We stare at each other for a minute.

"What's going on, Amber?"

Amber.

That's what's going on. And it's never going to be fixed.

I shake my head.

"Tell me," he demands. He hasn't moved at all, but his presence has shifted. He's intimidating now when he was so soft and relaxed and almost sweet before.

"There's nothing to tell."

"Yes, there is. And I need to know what it is."

I make a frustrated sound and flop over onto my back, closing my eyes and breathing deeply to calm the surge of fear that's risen inside me.

I need an excuse. Something. Anything to tell him that might explain why my mood has been changing so quickly lately.

Sad. He believes me to be sad.

What would make Amber sad?

"I guess maybe I've been thinking about my dad more lately," I say in a different tone.

"Why is that?"

"I don't know." Hit with a sudden brainstorm, I follow up on my tenuous excuse. "But I've been thinking... I've been wanting... Would it be okay if I start making jewelry?"

I have to turn my head to look at him since I need to see his expression.

It's surprised but thoughtful. He's taking me seriously. "I thought you said you don't do that."

Amber must have said that. She never got into the crafting aspect of the family business like I did.

"I didn't for a long time, but... I don't know... It's a connection to my family. My dad. And I was thinking maybe I want to start it up again."

"Of course you can make jewelry. You can do anything you want to do. What do you need from me?"

My heart is fluttering. For a different reason this time. "I'll need some supplies. And maybe I can set up a little corner here where I can work."

"Of course. Pick any space you want. You decorated the whole place except my office anyway. You can make any changes you want."

Well, that explains who was responsible for the decor of this place.

"Why don't you take the blue room? We don't need a second guest room since we never have any guests. Just call Gina about the furnishings you need, and she'll arrange for everything the way she did when you set up this place."

I have no idea who Gina is, but I can do a search of Amber's contacts and probably find her.

"Okay. Thank you." I'm flushed and beaming and a little shaky. So excited.

I can start working on jewelry again. It will give me something to do. And maybe I can actually start to feel like myself again.

"Why didn't you ask me before?"

"I wasn't sure what I wanted until right now."

His eyes are narrowed slightly, but he doesn't look

angry. Just focused. "I'd love to see what you make. I thought you had no interest in that at all."

"I didn't for a long time. But I'm thinking maybe I do now."

It's easy for me to find the correct Gina in Amber's contacts since she's the only one with that first name. I have no idea what her actual role or job position is, but I send her a quick text saying I want to make some changes to the furnishings in the apartment, and Gina calls me back almost immediately, excited to hear what I want to change.

In less than a week, the second guest room has been completely transformed into a studio for me—with a large worktable, a wall of drawers and shelving for supplies, a small desk, and a cozy seating area in one corner.

I love it. It's perfect. It's the kind of workspace I've always dreamed of. On the following Monday morning, I sit down to work for the first time in months.

Before I know it, it's midafternoon and I've been so absorbed I completely forgot about lunch.

I would probably continue working all day since it feels like being embraced by an old friend, but I've unfortunately got coffee scheduled with one of Amber's friends at four. I'm tempted to text and cancel, but this particular friend has been nagging me for two weeks about getting together, and I'm not sure how much longer I can hold her off.

It's time to get this over with. I take a shower, put on a stylish Amber outfit, then make my way to the trendy coffee shop where I've arranged to meet with Haley.

Any worries I might have about identifying her are assuaged when I step in through the door and an attractive redhead who looks around thirty immediately jumps up with a happy squeal and runs over to hug me.

In the month I've spent as Amber so far, I've never met anyone who appeared as genuinely pleased to see me as Haley. Plenty of women have poured on saccharine gushes —easily recognized as either fake or superficial—and quite a few men have flashed me looks of hot interest. But no one actually seems to know Amber for real or care about her.

So I'm shocked and rather bewildered by Haley's sincerely warm greeting.

We spend a few minutes on preliminary small talk, getting our cappuccinos and pastries and finding a two-person table near the window.

I wouldn't have gotten a cupcake had Haley not gotten one too. It ends up being a small mistake, as Haley appears surprised but delighted in what is clearly a change in habits for Amber. But I make up an easy excuse about feeling like indulging myself today, and she doesn't question it.

Following the strategy I've been practicing for weeks now, I ask her about what's going on in her life, letting the first half hour focus entirely on her and the small boutique she opened last year and her various dating experiences over the past couple of months. She's so openly nice that I'm actually interested in what she tells me of her life, so I ask a lot of questions and not only to fill the conversation in a way that's safe for me.

She's not one of those people who are happy to talk only about herself, however. So after a while she begins shifting the topic, asking about how I've been doing and what I've been up to lately.

Usually I can get away with a few vague replies about everything being the same and William doing well and staying busy. But Haley actually wants to know details.

I end up telling her about setting up the studio. She clearly knows about my family's connection to jewelry, and she's thrilled that I'm getting back to my roots. She asks a lot of insightful questions about the craft, and because I'm convinced she actually cares about the answers, I ramble on for a long time—talking more than I can remember with anyone since Amber and I were close.

"Oh, I'm so glad," Haley says at last. She's got a sprinkling of freckles on her nose and cheeks and lovely brown eyes. "And I'm so glad to hear William is supportive."

"He really is. I made one random comment to him and then suddenly everything was happening. I'm not used to people jumping in like that just to make me happy." My voice sounds a little too sappy, but surely that's appropriate when referring to my fiancé.

When I glance over, Haley has her head cocked. She's watching me with a warm kind of curiosity.

"What?" I demand, self-conscious by her expression.

"Nothing. You just seem... I don't know... different."

I swallow hard, hiding it with a smile. "You think so?"

"Yeah. If I didn't know better, I'd think you were a different person."

Oh shit.

"Well, I'm not."

"I know that. But still... Don't you think we just had the best conversation we've ever had."

"Yeah." My mind whirls, trying to sort through a way to handle this. "It's my fault. I know. I've been too standoffish, and I've done a lot of hiding behind the superficial. But I've been working on myself lately, and I want to do better. I'd like to have some real friends, and honestly you're my first choice."

Her face softens. Melts. "Really?"

"Yeah. I'm sorry if I didn't treat you right before, but I'm trying to do better now. If you still want to be friends."

"Of course I do! I've always wanted to be friends. I just never felt like I could make much progress. I'm so glad you've been working on yourself. It seems like things have maybe improved with William too?" She makes the last sentence a question with a slight uplift in her tone.

"Yeah. Yeah, they have."

"That's so good. I always thought he was a great guy, no matter how much he tries to hide it under that überprofessionalism. You two have a lot in common. Always trying to hide who you really are from the rest of the world."

"Y-yeah."

"But I've never seen you so clearly in love with him as you've been today. When you did nothing but complain about him, I always wondered…" She shakes her head.

"I was a bitch. You can just say it."

"I'd never say something like that. And you shouldn't say it about yourself either. You've just always been really closed off. A lot of people are that way."

"But not you." I can't help but smile at her.

She laughs. "Definitely not me." She glances at her phone. "I've got to get going soon, but let's set a time to get together later this week where we can hang out longer."

I pull up the calendar on my phone. "Sounds good to me. I don't have much going on this week, so what day works best for you?"

We plan a long lunch on Thursday, and I leave the coffee shop happier than when I came in.

Between getting back into work on jewelry and making an actual friend, I have a really good week. It goes quickly, and it's Friday before I know it.

William has been working long hours this week like normal, and there are some days when I only see him at bedtime and first thing in the morning.

Usually he works in his home office in the evenings rather than staying at work, but on Friday he must have meetings or a business dinner or something because he texts me around five and says he won't be home until late.

It shouldn't matter to me. It's not like we normally eat dinner together or hang out after work. But his text bothers me anyway. So much that, when I see it flash on my screen and read what it says, I don't even reply. It sits there on my phone like a pesky ache, drawing just a little too much of my attention as I make myself a small steak and roasted vegetables and try to focus on first a book and then a movie.

Finally, having the red notification of an unread text bothers me so much I pull it up. Read it again.

I'm stuck here until late today. Will be after eleven.

That's the first line of the message, but he left a space and added another three sentences that I couldn't see in the preview pop-up.

Every little thing is making me crazy today. No idea why. Pretty soon I'm going to knock heads together.

I giggle at the second half of the message. I don't know

why it tickles me, but it does. It isn't intimate or thoughtful or particularly meaningful. But it just feels so real. Like something normal to say to a partner about their day.

I tap out a reply. *I know the feeling. I've been in a mood all day today too. Hope you can wrap things up sooner than you think.*

I read my response over once and hit Send. Then read it again and wonder if the last sentence sounds too needy. Like I want him to come home soon.

I stress on it way too much as I see the three dots indicating he's in the midst of replying.

Then finally his text message pops up on my screen. *I'm trying. Feels like I've barely seen you this week.*

That's exactly how I feel myself, but I've been telling myself it's irrational. The previous weeks we've spent together haven't been different than this one. It's only on the weekends that I see him more. But I'm starting to feel his absence more and more on weekdays.

After waging a quick mental debate about how to reply, I end up saying, *Same here. See you when you get back.*

It's not exactly what I want to express, but the conversation is making me decidedly nervous, so it's probably safer to close it down.

I wait for a minute to see if he responds again, but he doesn't. There's no reason he would. I clearly ended the exchange.

But still...

I read over our texts several times, wishing I'd said things differently, until I finally groan and purposefully put down my phone.

I'm being ridiculous. It doesn't matter how I word every sentence in a few casual text messages. He's not going to be reading into things the way I do.

Men tend not to do that as much anyway, and it's not like he's hiding a huge secret like I am.

I take a bath, leaving my phone out of arm's reach, and then I climb into bed to read. I pick out an old favorite instead of trying new books, and this works better to occupy my mind.

It's almost ten when I hear sounds at the front door. I lower my book and look up to see William walking down the hall toward our bedroom.

"Hey," he says, scanning my face and position in a quick look. "You're in bed early."

"Yeah. I was just restless and grumpy, so I decided to read in bed. You got back earlier than you thought."

"I should have stayed longer, but my mood was further deteriorating so I figured it was better for everyone involved if I just come home." He looks tired and rumpled in his gray suit and loosened tie. His eyes rest on me almost wistfully. Then something twists on his face. "I won't bother you since you're—"

"I was killing time," I say, realizing he's about to make a retreat the minute after he got home. "I don't actually need to go to bed at nine o'clock. Have you eaten anything?"

He shakes his head.

"I've got leftovers from my dinner. I can fix them for you." I climb out of bed, quickly pulling down my camisole when it gets hiked up toward my breasts.

"You don't need to—"

"I just told you I've got nothing better to do. You look exhausted. It will take a few minutes to fix your food, so why don't you take a quick shower?"

"I can help you—"

"I don't need help. Take a shower. You'll feel better."

His mouth twitches up. "Kind of bossy tonight, aren't you?"

"Yes. I am. I've been looking for something to do, so I'm not going to let you take it away from me. Take a shower, and I'll get your dinner together." I try to keep my voice light so he won't know I'm fighting the urge to pet him, stroke him, take care of him.

He opens his mouth to say something but must rethink it. His mouth tightens. He swallows visibly. "Okay. Thanks."

He's taking off his jacket when I walk barefoot out of the bedroom, pulling up my pajama pants as I go since I'm pretty sure my panties are showing.

I do have plenty of leftover vegetables from my dinner, but I only grilled one small steak and I finished it. But there's another one in the refrigerator, so I take it out, pat it dry and salt it as I wait for the grill to heat up.

It doesn't take long to grill the steak. As it's resting afterward, I venture into the wine closet, hoping a good choice will miraculously occur to me. Red is best with steak. I know that much. But the nuances and variations are beyond me. I'm definitely wine illiterate, and for the first time in my life I wish I wasn't.

"See anything you like?" The familiar male voice comes from behind me. Unexpected. Making me jerk slightly.

"I don't know. I'm not very good at picking out wine, and I don't want to accidentally pick something super expensive."

"All the special stuff is on the top shelf. Anything else is fair game."

I turn my head to look at him. He must have kept his hair out of the spray since it's just a little damp on the edges. He's wearing a T-shirt and soft, thin black pajama pants that cling to his hips and legs in a tantalizing way.

He steps forward and reaches over my shoulder to wrap his hand around a bottle of Malbec. "This will go well with steak."

"Okay. That sounds good to me." I'm relieved by his taking care of the wine choice, but I'm also quite unsettled by his closeness. His body is brushing up against my back, and I really like how it feels.

He lingers longer than I would have expected, standing right behind me. It feels like he's looking at me, but I'm too nervous to turn my head again to check.

Then he finally steps back, and I follow him out of the closet. I finish putting his plate together, breathing slowly and telling myself to relax and get it together.

He pours out two glasses of red wine and offers me one. "You don't want anything to eat?"

"Nah, I had plenty earlier. But I'll definitely try this wine."

This decision evidently pleases him. He sits on one of the counter stools where I set up his plate, and I take the stool next to him.

I try not to watch him too closely as he cuts a piece of the steak and takes a bite.

He makes a low, guttural sound that's clearly pleasure as he chews. "This is amazing. Thanks."

"Sure. I had everything basically done, so it was easy."

"Everything you make is really good. I appreciate you leaving me so many leftovers."

I shrug, feeling my cheeks go pink as I focus steadily on my wineglass. "I like cooking, and it's hard to cook for just one."

"You've been cooking a lot lately. I didn't realize you liked it since you've never done it much before."

Shit. Yet another way I've changed Amber's habits.

I use the same excuse I've used before. "It's something new I'm trying. I'm not all that good at it."

"I beg to differ," he says before taking a big mouthful of roasted pepper and potato. "You're great at it."

"Oh. Well. Thanks." I take a slow sip of wine and try to turn the conversation. "So tell me about work. What was so annoying today?"

He accepts the shift in topic and tells me about what he was trying to get done and how other people weren't cooperating. He clearly recognizes that a lot of the problem was his own mood and not everyone else's complete incompetence. He relaxes as he eats and talks. He still looks tired as he finishes his plate, but he doesn't look nearly so battered.

It feels like a job well done. Like I've done something to help him. Take care of him. We keep chatting as we finish our wine, and then I suggest he come to bed early instead of going to his office to work some more.

To my surprise, he does exactly that.

I'm nervous again as he climbs into the bed beside me, smelling like soap and toothpaste and the slightest hint of red wine. He's looking at me. Not lustfully or aggressively. But in a strangely focused way. Like he's waiting to see what I'll do.

What I want to do is drag him over on top of me, but I restrain the impulse. "We can watch a movie or something if you're not ready to sleep yet."

"Sure. That's a good idea." He doesn't look disappointed, but he lets out a long breath, like he's willing himself to let go of some sort of tension.

We find an old movie that both of us like and start playing it.

William is asleep before it's halfway over, and I barely make it to the end.

I wake up a few hours later flushed and breathless and aroused.

At first I'm in that fuzzy blur on the edge of sleep, aware of little else than the needy throbbing of my body and a hot weight on my back.

It's pressing into me, pushing me into the mattress, but it isn't unpleasant or claustrophobic. I love the feeling. Need it. Want more of it.

"Please." The word is soft and raspy. Although I feel the sound in my throat, there's no way I'm the one who said it.

There's a huffing sound from behind me, and I suddenly realize that it's William.

William is on top of me. Making me feel this way.

His weight is hard, and something even harder is poking against my butt.

"Please!" That's me again, still soft but almost desperate. I raise my hips slightly so I can feel him more intensely.

He huffs again and makes a clumsy little thrust against my bottom. It's instinctive. Primal, not purposeful. I know it even through the hungry haze of my brain.

I gasp at the tight clench of pleasure the move prompts in me.

William makes a mumbling sound and thrusts a few more times.

He's asleep.

I always sleep on my side, facing away from him, and he usually does the same. But he must have rolled over at some point as he was sleeping and rolled on top of me, pushing me over onto my stomach.

I can't imagine another scenario where we would have ended up like this without either of us doing it purposefully.

But it feels so good. My body craves even more. I want him to keep thrusting, tear off my clothes, push that erection inside me until both of us find release.

I'm not asleep anymore, but he still is. That means I have to somehow stop this. It feels like sex to me, but he's not even conscious of doing it.

It's wrong. I've got to make it stop.

The guilt is enough to distract me from the carnal urges. I scoot closer to the edge of the bed, trying to slide out from under him.

He turns onto his side, taking me with him, and uses

one arm to drag me closer. Snug against his body. He pumps his hips with a low, primitive groan.

Oh fuck. I'm about to lose it. I want it so much.

Panting loudly, I use all the will I have left to move his arm and pull away.

He resists, trying to pull me back, but the jerky move must finally wake him up.

He makes a weird, throaty sound, and the tension in his body shifts unmistakably.

He grows very still.

I'm still on my side, clinging to the edge of the bed. Slammed with waves of heat and embarrassment and confusion, I keep my eyes closed and try to even out my breathing.

He needs to think I'm asleep. That's the only way we're going to get out of this mortifying situation.

I feel the slightest touch on my shoulder, like he reached out with only his fingertips.

I still don't move. He's got to think I'm still sleeping.

Then he mutters very softly, "Fuck. Oh fuck."

With a stifled groan, he gets out of bed and walks quickly into the bathroom. I hear the door click and let out a raspy sigh.

That was torture. An erotic kind of torture.

I hear the shower turn on and can only imagine what he's doing in there.

Unfortunately, I do imagine it. I picture him in there,

pumping himself with his hand until he releases with one of those primal groans.

I slide my hand between my legs and rub myself off to the mental visuals. I'm already so turned on that it takes almost no time at all for me to come.

I pant against the pillow as my body relaxes afterward, but my mind is still in an uproar.

How did I ever get into this situation? It's ridiculous.

William thinks I'm my sister. If he wants someone, it must be her.

5

THE NEXT MORNING, WILLIAM WAKES UP BEFORE I DO.

It's Saturday, and for once he doesn't go into his office. He's working from home when I get up at just before nine.

He comes into the kitchen to get another cup of coffee as I'm sitting at the island with my coffee and my phone. He greets me in a normal manner, and I do the same.

There's no mention of what happened last night. He's acting like it never happened, and I pretend I'm not even aware.

It's a relief. Almost entirely a relief. And if a tiny part of me is disappointed, I simply don't listen to that small voice.

We have a cocktail party to attend this evening, so I have to prep myself mentally for the public outing. I start a couple of hours before we need to leave so I won't be rushed getting dressed. I have a long shower and take my time with my hair, pulling it into a smooth chignon with a few loose strands framing my face so it looks a little softer. Then I spend longer than normal with my makeup, making my eyes smoky and my lips red.

I'm quite pleased with the results. I search Amber's closet for a dress to wear, bored with the interminable whites and creams and pale grays she prefers. I finally land on a simple, elegant sheath in a silvery green that molds my figure.

What I would give for a bright color to wear.

I'm picking out jewelry when William comes out from the bathroom, freshly showered and wearing the black pants and white dress shirt of his suit.

He pulls to a stop and stares at me for several seconds.

I glance down at myself. "Am I okay?"

He clears his throat. "Gorgeous. You look gorgeous."

My cheeks warm. I focus down at an emerald pendant on a gold chain I'm holding. Our dad designed it for our mom, and Amber must have kept it after he died. "Oh. Good. Thanks."

William is still standing in the middle of the floor, barefoot and holding a silver tie. His eyes are running up and down my body.

Self-conscious, I turn toward the mirror and place the pendant at the base of my throat, reaching around to clip the chain in the back.

I'm so awkward that I fumble with the clasp. After a

few seconds, William steps over and does it for me. His fingers brush against my skin, making me shiver.

He's watching me in the mirror.

I dart several quick looks up, meeting his eyes in the reflection. "What?" I finally ask.

"Nothing. It just feels like..." He gives his head a shake.

"Like what?"

"Like I've never seen you before." His voice is very thick.

Oh shit. "Oh." I take a ragged breath. "Well, you have."

"Yeah."

He returns to normal after that, pulling on his tie, jacket, socks, shoes, and watch. We're ready to go on time, and neither of us says anything at all.

I've been to a few different parties now, so they're not quite as intimidating as they were at first.

I've learned to read William's expressions as we wander around and mingle, so now I can figure out which ones he likes and which ones he doesn't. The ones he likes, I spend more time talking to, doing my best to be genuine and get to know them. With the ones he doesn't, I'm coolly courteous and don't bother sharing any of myself with them.

This is his world. Not mine. So there's little point in my

wasting my time and emotional energy on people who aren't worth it.

It feels like he's watching me more than normal tonight. Maybe I really do look better than usual, and he's simply stunned by the transformation.

Hopefully it's not more than that. Hopefully he doesn't see something in me that's not in Amber. Surely he won't start suspecting after all this time.

He keeps a hand on the small of my back as we circulate, and I wish I didn't like how it feels there so much. Like a gentle claim of ownership. Entitlement.

At one point, as we finish a conversation with an older couple, he cups my face with one hand and leans down to kiss me softly. It's light. Brief. Completely appropriate for a crowd.

But it still causes a shiver of pleasure to run up and down my spine, so intense I lose my breath.

"What was that for?" I ask rather stupidly, blinking up at him.

"That was because I wanted to kiss you."

"Oh." My eyes are wide, and my cheeks are flushed. I have no idea what to say or what to do.

He's not acting like he usually does, but that could mean so many different things.

I have no idea what's going on.

His mouth twitches up, and he uses his finger to trace a

line along my jaw and over to my mouth. He's going to say something. I'm sure he's going to say something.

And I desperately want to hear what he's going to say.

But someone drops a plate across the room, startling me and drawing our attention. Then the moment is gone.

We move on to more mingling. While William is talking to a tedious business associate I remember from the garden party, I notice a familiar face recently arrived.

Haley, looking gorgeous with her red hair loose and that warm smile on her face.

She greets me enthusiastically from across the room, and I make my excuses so I can walk over to her.

She hugs me like we're best friends and introduces me to her date, whom she promptly tells to go get them drinks and snacks.

While he's gone, she says, "Looks like things are going really well with William."

I blink in surprise. "What?"

She gestures toward where William is still talking to that same man—or rather, letting the other man talk while he nods as if he's interested. "I saw the two of you when I came in. Talk about electricity crackling in the air."

I giggle nervously. "It wasn't like that."

"Oh, yes, it was. I'm really happy the two of you have warmed up."

"What do you mean?"

"I mean, I tried to be supportive when you told me

about your arrangement, but it just didn't seem like a good idea to marry for mostly practical reasons. Sure, people do it all the time, but I can't imagine it leads to real happiness. And I wanted you both to be happy. But I don't mind admitting I was totally wrong. You guys have really got something going now. Which is crazy because for a while I couldn't see any chemistry between the two of you at all. But now..." She grins.

I'm flushing hotly. "It's not like that."

"Oh, yes, it is." She glances over my shoulder. "He's looking at you right now, and I swear he could swallow you whole."

It takes every ounce of my control not to look back and see William's expression right now.

"I'm happy for you," Haley says again, and it's impossible not to believe that she means it. "It doesn't happen for everyone. We can't all find someone who fits so perfectly. So don't you dare let him go now that you found him."

I gulp. "I... I won't."

A few hours later, our car lets us out in front of our building, and we walk together through the lobby and to the private elevator that leads up to our place.

My feet are killing me, and I have to fight not to limp. I'm not sure if I'm entirely successful since William moves a hand to the small of my back in that supportive gesture he's been using all evening.

I like how the light pressure feels. I like how he looks, how he smells, how he feels beside me, and I can't help but wonder what it would be like to have a man in my life —one who is really with me. For so long, I've prided myself on my self-sufficiency. I don't need a man to be okay. But there are some things about it that are really nice.

We've gotten into the lobby when I notice someone in a dark, inexpensive suit standing across from the main entrance. He's in his forties—with dark hair, dark eyes, and a pleasant face. I recognize him immediately.

He's a police detective from back in Houston. Detective Curtis. The one who is friends with Montaigne. I'm positive that he and his official resources are the main reason I could never really get away from my stalker.

My heart leaps into my throat, and I'm washed with a wave of ice cold. I glance away from him immediately, as if my eyes accidentally flickered in his direction. I keep walking with William.

But Detective Curtis knows me. He *knows* me.

"Jade," he calls out, straightening up as soon as he sees me.

I don't turn around. My eyes are on the guard in front of me, the one manning the private elevator.

"Ms. Delaney," Curtis calls, even louder. He must be

approaching quickly since his voice is much closer than it was. "Jade Delaney!"

William stops and turns around to frown at Curtis. One of the security staff, in a matter of three seconds, is standing between William and the other man.

"I'm not Jade," I say, my voice a little raspy from fear. My hands are shaking, but I manage to hide them by twisting them together. "I'm Amber Delacourte."

Curtis stops abruptly and stares at me in disbelief.

"Who exactly are *you*?" William demands. His cold, condescending tone is incredibly comforting.

Curtis starts to reach into his jacket pocket but is forcefully prevented from doing so by the guard.

"I'm a police detective," he chokes out, clearly surprised and outraged by such manhandling. "I was going to show my credentials."

At a nod from William, the guard releases Curtis, and he presents his credentials to William. "I'm from Houston. I came to DC to look for Jade Delaney."

William glances over the credentials and then looks back at Curtis with a shrug. "I don't know who Jade Delaney is. But this is my fiancée, Amber Delacourte." He appears defensive, almost protective. And I can't help but appreciate it—even if he believes he's protecting Amber and not me. Besides, William's interference has given me time to catch my breath and pull myself together.

"Jade is probably my sister," I volunteer, since I have to

admit it now. "She must have changed her last name when she left home. I didn't know what she changed it to, but it must be her you're looking for."

Curtis's dark eyebrows draw together dubiously. "Your sister? You look exactly alike."

"We're twins." I'm uncomfortably aware of William's surprised, observant eyes on my face. I pull Amber's driver's license out of my purse and hand it to Curtis as proof of my identity since I don't think he'll believe me otherwise. "Is she all right? I haven't talked to her in years."

"Actually," Curtis says, evidently accepting that I'm Amber and handing the license back after studying it closely. "She's not. She's in some trouble and she's disappeared. We're trying to find her. I managed to trace her back to you and was hoping you might know where she is."

Some trouble.

That's what he's saying.

The only trouble I've ever gotten into is being stalked by Montaigne, and now this man is making it sound like I'm the bad guy.

I really can't believe this. Montaigne somehow got a police detective to come all the way to DC to track me down.

I shake my head, doing my best to keep my face composed and my eyes steady. "I don't. We had a falling out a long time ago and haven't talked to each other since.

It's been like nine or ten years. How exactly is she in trouble?"

I really want to know what his story is going to be.

Curtis glances from me to William to the guard to the doorman. "Maybe we can talk about this somewhere more private?"

I don't want to bring him up to the apartment since I want to get rid of him as soon as possible. But I'm not sure how to refuse without looking suspicious, and I'm about to agree when William speaks over me.

"I don't think so. You can talk to her here for a few minutes. If it goes on too long, I'm calling a lawyer."

I can't suppress a flicker of gratitude as I look up at William's handsome, unmoving face. He looks like an aristocrat from a Merchant-Ivory film in his suit and innate elegance. But he's a consummate professional, and he probably has a whole law firm on retainer.

I put a hand on his arm and say, "I don't need a lawyer right now. I'm happy to talk to him down here for a minute or two." I emphasize the last words to make it clear I'm not overriding William's decision to not invite Curtis into our home. "Will you please tell me why my sister is in trouble?"

"We were investigating her for a number of reasons, but she disappeared on us."

"How did she disappear?" I reassure myself that the

breathlessness in my voice will merely sound like worry for my sister.

He shrugs. "We aren't sure how she managed. We can't seem to track her down, so we're assuming she had some help."

"Maybe she was killed!" I raise a hand to cover my mouth, not having to fake my astonishment. The absolute gall of this man.

"We don't think so. We think she ran away and that she had help."

"Well, she didn't get any help from me."

Curtis gives me a faintly exasperated look. "You're sure you haven't heard from your sister recently? Maybe she tried to make contact, but you didn't realize—"

"I would know if I'd heard from her. I haven't been in touch with her for nine years. Sorry."

"Can you think of anyone else she might have turned to for help?"

"I'm not sure. All our friends as kids have scattered, but I doubt she stayed connected to them. She cut ties with everyone when she left home. I have no idea who she might be friends with now."

"Okay." He looks like he's going to suggest something, but then his eyes flick over to William and he evidently changes his mind. "Would you mind if I get in touch with you again if we have further questions?"

I'm about to agree when William says, "Call first. Don't show up like this again."

I can't help but smile up at William as Curtis walks away. It's really nice—I have to admit—not having to face the detective alone.

I haven't had anyone on my side in a really long time.

He smiles back. For a moment, our eyes linger and something warm swells up in my chest.

But then we get on the elevator and the emotional response subsides. I feel weak and a little trembly. Overall, I handled things pretty well, but there's always the chance that I've given something away. To Curtis. Or to William.

"I didn't know you had a twin sister," William murmurs, slanting his eyes over at me as the elevator doors slid shut.

"She's not part of my life anymore. She hates me."

I try to prepare my answers in case William asks questions, but he doesn't. He's quiet for the rest of the way up to the apartment.

And then, like normal, he disappears into his office to work.

I change out of the elegant dress I wore to the cocktail party. Since I'm tired and upset by the confrontation with

Detective Curtis downstairs, I take my bath early in an attempt to relax.

I light candles, turn on soft music, and fill the large tub with hot, lavender-and-honey-scented water before I get in to soak. As my body relaxes, my mind lets go of its defenses unexpectedly.

I start to cry.

For the past twenty minutes, ever since I saw Detective Curtis waiting in the lobby, I've been working in very intense panic mode, every sense and reflex primed for fight or flight.

For the past four weeks, ever since I turned into Amber, I've been living a lie, constantly on guard against being found out.

For the past eight months, ever since I had that twenty-minute conversation with Montaigne about the custom pendant for his mother, I've been scanning every crowd, always looking over my shoulder, waiting for him to make his final move.

For the past nine years, ever since I left home, I've been trying to run away from anyone who might make me feel and from the girl I was before—the one who always trusted and always ended up hurt.

All of it is just too hard. I don't want to do it anymore.

I cry for a long time in the tub, making sure to stifle the sound although it's a little early for William to emerge from his office. When I've cried myself out, the water is starting to cool, so I drain the tub and get out, drying myself off with the thick towel I heated on the fancy towel warmer.

I put on a set of new pajamas I bought last week. They're made of this thick, soft knit I love—smoky lavender with loose pants and a sleeveless top. I cover them with a long sweater and pour a glass of red wine. Then, still restless and uneasy, I walk outside onto the large terrace, stand near the high railing, and stare out at the expansive view of the city in the evening.

I can just leave. Finally give up on Amber, who clearly isn't interested in a genuine reconciliation. Forget about this crazy scheme and find a little town where no one knows me. Get a job at a diner or a bookstore and start life again.

But I don't have the resources to establish a new identity, which means Montaigne will eventually find me, unless I can somehow live on cash without setting up a bank account, car registration, and utilities.

It doesn't sound feasible.

I can go to another law enforcement agency and tell them my story. Hope they'll take me seriously. Pray they don't have anyone bribable in their ranks.

Or I can keep doing what I'm doing.

Those are the only options I can think of.

I wish there was someone I could confide in, someone who I could turn to for support and comfort. I suddenly miss Amber—the Amber I remember from our childhood —so much my chest constricts. For a moment, I can't even breathe.

I fight the tears since I've already cried more than I ever allow myself. But I'm only starting to regain my breath when a voice from behind me surprises me so much I jerk and slop my wine.

"Are you all right?" William asks, having joined me on the terrace without my realizing it.

I manage to compose my face and turn around, wiping my hand on the sweater since wine sloshed on it. "Yeah. I'm fine. Just tired."

William's eyes are dark in the glow of the terrace lights, and they're fixed on my face. "You don't look fine."

"I am." I'm slightly impatient. This man normally stays distracted by work, so it's annoying and troubling when he suddenly decides to pry into my business like this. I turn back toward the view. Away from him. "I'm fine."

He steps over so he's beside me next to the terrace railing. "Tell me about your sister."

I knew this question would come up soon. "There's not much to tell. Her name is Jade. Jade and Amber. Nice, huh? We're twins. She's... I'm a couple of hours older. We're not that much alike."

"Curtis said you were identical."

"We are. I mean, we're identical twins. We look alike, but we're different in every other way." I suddenly realize this is an important moment for me. If William believes Amber and I are interchangeable, he might start to suspect why the woman he knows as Amber has been acting so different lately. I can't let that happen. "We're not exactly alike. There are some differences. But, yeah, we're twins. It's been ages since I've seen her."

"You told Curtis it's been nine years since you've talked to her. So you haven't spoken to her since you were eighteen?"

I frown, wishing William wasn't so good at remembering details. "Yes. That's right. She ran away from home. Left me and my dad."

"Why did she run away?"

I shrug.

"You must know something."

With a sniff, I say lightly, "Our dad was... difficult. She felt trapped by him, I think. So she left."

He's quiet for a long time. Then, "And she never tried to stay in touch even with you?"

I shrug again, trying not to squirm.

"Did something happen between the two of you?"

"Why does it matter?"

He makes an impatient sound. "Because you've clearly been crying, and I've never seen you cry in all the time I've known you. What happened between the two of you hurt you, so I want to know what it is."

He thinks he's talking to Amber. Not me. He sounds so

defensive for Amber. Not me.

To him, Jade will be the bad guy.

I'll be the bad guy.

It takes a few seconds for me to get my voice to work. "Yeah. We had a fight. She didn't... She... I didn't want her to leave everything. To be someone different. She even changed her name. It felt like a... betrayal. Of me. So I didn't react... I could have done better."

He reaches out to cup one of my cheeks with his big, warm hand. "What did you do, sweetheart?"

There's a tug of feeling in my chest at the endearment, at how much I want to hear it. From him.

But he's talking to Amber.

I should make up a story right now—throw myself under the bus. Tell him how terrible Jade was to me. Something to adequately explain our long separation and my emotions right now.

But I can't make myself do it. I can't betray anyone else, not even myself, by telling another lie.

It's so terrible—all of it—my vision blurs over. I close my eyes.

"Tell me," he says, hoarse and demanding.

I shake my head and pull away from his hand, turning around so he can't see me contorting my face to keep from crying. "I don't want to talk about it." I force the words out, wobbly and unnatural. I set down my wineglass since I'm not sure how long I'll be able to keep it steady.

William is silent, but he doesn't go away. He simply stands there, and I can feel his eyes on me even though I'm turned away from him.

The evening air is cool, and a breeze blows against my hot face and raw eyes, blowing loose strands of my hair that escaped from the clip I secured it with before my bath. I can smell William beside me—that light, clean, expensive scent that is, like the man himself, both masculine and sophisticated. He's still wearing the fancy suit he wore to the party, although he's taken off the jacket and loosened his tie. I can hear him breathe.

His presence should have helped me control my emotions since I can't afford to break down in front of him, but for some reason it makes it worse. My vision still hasn't fully cleared, and now my shoulders start to shake.

It's humiliating. And dangerous. But I can't seem to not sob.

"Come here," William murmurs, a thickness to his voice that's only occasionally there. He puts a hand on my shoulder and turns me around.

I lose it. Shatter. I start to cry for real and let him pull me against his chest. His body is hard, lean, and warm, and his arms are strong around me. It feels like he cares about me. Like he wants to comfort me.

Like he's holding me together.

Whether it's real or not, it changes things. I don't feel alone anymore.

Eventually my sobs subside, but I keep my face buried in his white dress shirt. It feels so good to have him hold me like this. Plus I'm embarrassed by the breakdown—don't want to see his expression when I pull away.

He's still got his arms around me as he asks softly, "Please tell me what you did, sweetheart."

I did what I needed to do at eighteen—to protect myself and be my own person. And I spent years pleading for Amber to forgive me, to be in my life again, to understand why I made the choices I made.

I met her a month ago, still hoping that we could reconnect for real.

But that's not what she wanted. It may never be what she wants. I might be broken, but she's even more broken than me.

"I... I lost her. I love her, but she's lost to me—and I'm afraid it might be forever."

I don't know why I tell him this. The final bitter truth of my heart. Why it needs to be said. Why it feels safe for him to hear it.

But the words come out, and there's no way I can stop them.

He runs his hand down my back in what's almost a caress. He doesn't say anything at all.

Finally I don't have a choice about pulling out of the hug. I straighten up and wipe the last of the tears from my face, darting him a self-conscious look.

His expression is quiet and thoughtful, and I'm not quite sure what it means. "How long has it been since you've cried?"

I look down. "I'm not sure." Since I don't know when Amber last cried, I can't make a definitive statement, but he said earlier he's never known her to cry, so she's clearly not any more of a crier than me. "Sorry about that."

"Don't be sorry. You don't always have to hide."

I suck in a quick breath and glance up, but he reveals nothing but that same watchful quietness. He doesn't appear suspicious or like he's playing games with me. He's talking about Amber. He won't know he managed to capture Jade perfectly in so few words.

I mumble something incoherent and look back out toward the city.

William stands beside me, also gazing at the cityscape, for a really long time. We don't say anything.

After a while, the silence starts to make me uncomfortable. Since I'm more controlled now and need a way to move past the emotional interlude, I say, "I thought you might work late this evening."

William glances over at me, looking faintly surprised. But his mouth is twitching in the way I've learned to recognize is amusement. "It's late enough," he murmurs, a different sort of thickness entering his voice.

My breath hitches as I stare up at him. My body starts to hum in response to the texture in his voice and the soft heat that has sparked in his eyes. I can't look away from him, and a heady tension tightens in my chest and between my legs.

He somehow gets closer, although neither of us appears to have moved. He raises a hand to cup my face again, and this time his thumb gently caresses my cheek where the track of a tear is. "Fuck, you're beautiful." His eyes are devouring me. "Beautiful and... and alive somehow."

I gasp and sway toward him instinctively, completely lost in the sensations and the feel of his intimate regard. Summoning what I can of my control, I say breathlessly, "William, I..." I trail off, completely unable to think of a way to end this encounter the way I know I should.

My heart is racing, and my body has flushed hot. William is leaning down toward me, and I want him to.

I *want* him.

When his lips close on mine, a rush of deep pleasure ripples through me. My arms twine around his neck, and I press my body against his. He unclips my hair and then tangles his fingers in the loose waves as they fall down over my back. His mouth moves against mine eagerly, urgently. Then his tongue starts to tease.

Overwhelmed by feelings and sensation, I open to the advance of his tongue, moaning low in my throat as the pleasure deepens even further. My body pulses with growing desire, and I claw shamelessly at his shirt.

I want to feel him. I want to feel all of him.

He pushes me back against the railing, so I'm trapped between it and his hard body. One of his hands slips down to my bottom and presses my pelvis firmly against his. He's already hard, the bulge in his trousers pressing deliciously against my middle. I tear my mouth away from his and gasp desperately for air, my arousal aching so deeply I can't help but grind myself against his hip.

My head falls back, and I moan with pleasure as William lowers his mouth to suck on the pulse at my throat.

Suddenly, through the fog of need and desire, I remember that William thinks I'm Amber. He's making out with Amber, not me.

He wants Amber, not me.

"William, wait." I stiffen as I'm hit by the painful realization. "Stop."

He groans in frustration, but his body grows still. With effort, he lifts his head from my neck. "Why?" His cheeks are flushed, and he's holding his body as stiffly as I am.

I try to think, try to come up with a convincing excuse. There's no reason William shouldn't be able to make love to his fiancée—except I'm not really his fiancée.

"I thought you might really want this. Me." His voice is still hoarse with desire. But there's something else there too. Something almost hurt.

I can't allow it. Not when I'm the cause of it. "I do. I do

want this. But I'm... I've been... I'm still doing a lot of thinking." I have to ease my body away from his since I'm fighting the urge to rub myself against him. "I'm trying to do better, but I don't think I'm quite there yet. I was hoping... if it's all right with you... I was hoping I could have a little more time to work through things before we... before we... since sex complicates things even more."

William's brown eyes bore into me, like he's seeing into my soul. I don't think my excuse is a great one, but it's somewhat plausible. He might buy it.

After a long moment of scrutiny, something on his face changes. It seems to relax. Then, inexplicably, one corner of his mouth twitches. "I understand." He pushes my messy hair back from my face and then gently caresses my cheek with his thumb. "I can wait."

I let out a sigh of relief, reminding myself that the softness in his eyes isn't for me. "Thank you. I know it's not fair to you."

"Don't worry about it." He leans down to kiss me softly. "I'm a patient man. I'm going to take a shower."

I smile at him as he leaves the terrace. Then I pick up my wine and turn back to stare out at the city.

I wonder if William will be heartbroken when he discovers what Amber and I have done to him.

One thing was certain. He deserves a lot better than he's been given.

6

As I get back home on a Thursday evening, I'm hungry, tired, and restless.

Earlier this afternoon, I had to go to a meeting of a museum board that Amber serves on, which ended up being the hardest hurdle I've tackled in the month and a half I've spent as Amber. Over the past two weeks, ever since the cocktail party, I've had several lunches with Amber's friends and a couple of dinners with William and his business acquaintances. I've also started attending a trendy martial arts class with Haley.

All those activities have been easier than the board meeting, which consisted of ten virtual strangers who all know Amber well and a complicated set of conflicting agendas that I'm utterly clueless about.

The preliminary communications made it clear this

wasn't a meeting that Amber could legitimately miss. So I dressed in an ivory suit with a dark green scarf and four-inch heels, and I steeled my nerves enough to make the effort.

I successfully maneuvered through the two-hour meeting, mostly by saying as little as possible and going along with the general consensus about the issues that needed deciding. But I was brutally on edge for most of the day, so I'm exhausted when I finally get home.

Right away I take a shower and change into pale gray knit pants and a matching sweater, wishing that Amber owned something that more closely resembled baggy sweats. Then I walk down the hall and pause at the closed door of William's study.

The past two weeks have been pretty good with William. I see him more often than I did before since he's started coming home earlier from work and he's had more dinners and cocktail parties on his schedule that I'm supposed to attend with him. Seeing him a lot more might have been stressful and difficult, but it hasn't been.

At all.

Ever since our confrontation with Detective Curtis and the conversation and kiss on the terrace afterward, William seems to have relaxed in an inexplicable way. He's evidently finally accepted the changes in my behavior. He hasn't questioned me about acting strange, and he hasn't appeared so distant or suspicious. I'm relieved—partly because I finally feel safer in my role, and partly because I like William and it feels better when we're getting along.

He'll never be an easy man. He's guarded, ambitious, driven by the ghosts of Worthings past. Reluctant to ever be vulnerable.

He's like me in that way. I can understand him. I've spent years of my life refusing to let anyone in, refusing to let anyone get close enough to hurt me. But it still vaguely annoys me as I stand in front of William's closed office door. If one of the security staff hadn't mentioned how early he got home today, I wouldn't even know William is in there right now.

Surely it would make sense to at least say hello at the end of the day. But his damned door is always closed—he even locks it when he leaves. I don't for a moment imagine he's hiding deep, dark secrets inside. It's simply his private sanctum, the place he can escape from the rest of the world.

And that world includes me.

Or Amber, rather.

With a sigh, I continue down the hall. I'm hungry and need something for dinner. I don't feel like ordering in, so I search the kitchen to see what there is I can make without too much hassle.

I find some lovely fresh shrimp and decide that will do

fine. I collect basil, pine nuts, parmesan, and olive oil and make some pesto in the fancy food processor. Then I put water on to boil for the pasta and heat up the stovetop grill.

I lay everything out on the counter, still feeling that strange restlessness I've been experiencing since I got home today.

I'm used to being alone, used to being by myself. But somehow knowing that William is working in the other room—just as alone as I am—makes me feel worse. Makes me feel lonely.

Before I can talk myself out of it, I stride back down the hall toward William's study. There, I knock firmly on the door, my heart beating a little faster.

The worst he can do is tell me to leave him alone. Then I can be justifiably annoyed with him and enjoy the evening on my own.

"It's open," he calls out, his voice muffled by the door but still sounding vaguely surprised. "Come in."

I swing the door open and stand on the threshold, staring blankly into his office.

I've never seen it before, and I'm genuinely surprised by how different it looks from the rest of the apartment. Instead of glossy marble, white upholstery, sleek lines, and minimalistic accessories, his home office has wide-planked hardwood floors in a dark brown, big traditional furniture, antique Asian rugs, oil paintings, and one wall covered entirely with bookshelves. The decor is so unexpected that I stand stupidly and blink at it.

"Is everything all right?" He's peering at me with concern from behind the computer on the desk. He's still wearing the dark suit he put on this morning, and there's an obvious question on his face.

I pull it together and smile at him. "Yeah. Sorry to interrupt. I was just making dinner and wondered if you wanted any."

For some reason, it bothers me that he's still wearing his tie, even working by himself at home. Doesn't the man ever unwind? Doesn't he ever relax?

He stares at me for a moment, blinking once.

I drop my eyes, suddenly self-conscious. "It's no big deal if you're too busy. But there's plenty if you're hungry."

"Sure," William says at last, closing out something on his computer and then standing up. "Thanks."

I'm even more self-conscious when he falls into step with me as we leave the office and head toward the kitchen. But that's ridiculous. William and I are supposed to be engaged. This should be a perfectly normal situation.

There's no reason to feel like we're on a first date.

I distract myself from my inappropriate responses by asking William to find us a bottle of wine as I put the shrimp on the grill and drop the fresh angel-hair pasta in the boiling water.

He comes out of the wine closet with a nice bottle of

chardonnay. Uncorks it and pours out two glasses. Then he helps me by turning the shrimp while I drain the pasta and then toss it with the pesto. We work easily together, and he doesn't appear to think anything is strange about our interaction. Occasionally it feels like he's watching me, but every time I check, his eyes are focused on something else.

I don't want dinner to feel awkward or formal, so I suggest we eat in the media room. William thinks this is a perfectly good idea, and it's not long until we're set up there with our dinner.

I turn on a news channel, but we don't end up needing the distraction. He asks me about my museum board meeting, and I give him a rundown, trying to make the otherwise boring meeting more interesting by highlighting the ongoing argument between two snotty attendees.

I relax at the sound of his warm chuckle, and it seems natural to ask him about his day as well. I'm pleased when he starts telling me more about the restructuring and transition of the Worthing companies.

I'm genuinely interested in what he says and ask a lot of detailed questions so I can get a better handle on it.

Before I know it, the food is gone and we've finished the bottle of wine. William gets us some sorbet from the kitchen, and bored with news, I flip over to an old Alfred Hitchcock film.

I'm wrapped up in a throw in the corner of the couch

when William returns with the sorbet. He's incredibly attractive and much less intimidating than normal since he's taken off his shoes, tie, and jacket. He still smells better than any man has the right to smell—that mingling of masculine and expensive that makes my belly twist. I like the look in his brown eyes too. Soft and warm, like he's actually enjoying himself.

The movie is one I like, but the long day catches up with me unexpectedly. I drift off to sleep before the first hour is over.

I wake up a couple of hours later, groggy and content. I blink a few times, not really sure where I am but remarkably comfortable.

The first thing I see is William, who's sitting on the other end of the sofa. He seems to have been watching me because his eyes are on my face. I smile up at him blurrily.

He smiles back, his watchful expression transforming into something much softer.

"Sorry," I mumble. "Did I miss the movie?"

"You missed the end of that one and most of a second one." The corner of his lips twitches slightly.

"Oh." I blink and try to get my mind to work. A glance at the clock shows it's after eleven. "You should have woken me up."

"Why would I wake you up?" he asks, still looking like he's amused.

With a pang of nervous self-consciousness, I sit up and pat at my hair. "Are you laughing at my hair?"

He laughs low in his throat. "Of course I'm not laughing at your hair." He reaches over and brushes my hair back from my face, his palm lingering on my cheek. "You're beautiful."

My breath hitches for a different reason now. I lean toward him instinctively, unthinkingly.

He kisses me gently, almost questioningly. The brush of his lips sends shivers of pleasure down my spine, but he pulls away before I can respond.

"The Bolshoi ballet is in town next weekend. Will you go with me on Friday next week?"

My lips part slightly. My mind is still fuzzy from sleep and from pleasure at the kiss, but something about his tone makes the question sound significant. I have no idea why going to the ballet would be significant, and I have no reason to refuse.

"Of course. Sounds lovely."

His eyes are unusually soft, almost fond. I have to remind myself that he's looking that way at Amber, not at me.

It's like cold water dashed over my warm contentment. I really have to be more careful than this.

Suddenly afraid I'm not being Amber-like enough, I add with a flirtatious smile, "I'll have to buy a new dress for the ballet."

His lips twitch again. "I'll look forward to seeing it."

I stare at my reflection in the full-length, tri-fold mirror in the loft studio of a trendy local designer.

The evening gown I'm wearing has been pinned so it fits me perfectly. It's a long white column sheath with a graceful drape of fabric over one shoulder that gives it a faintly Greek flavor. The dress is elegant, flattering, and sophisticated—and perfectly characteristic of Amber's taste in clothes. I'm surprised by how good I look in it since white isn't a color I'd ever wear by choice.

The dress is beautiful, stylish, classy... and kind of boring.

"It's perfect," says one of the designer's assistants, an effusive young man named Reid. "I knew it would be perfect for you, Ms. Delacourte. It's exactly you!"

I've never been to a private fitting with a designer before, but Amber must have done this fairly often when she needed an outfit for an important occasion since Reid talks as if we're familiar with each other. "Yeah." I try to suppress a sigh. "I suppose it is."

The dress is certainly Amber. And I'm supposed to be Amber. So this is probably the dress I should choose.

"Would you like to try on something else?" Reid asks, evidently seeing something lacking in my expression.

"Maybe. I do love this, especially the Greek look of it. But I don't know... I'm feeling like it might be nice to have a change of pace. Maybe something that's not white?"

There's no way I can get away with wearing a dress of crimson or emerald since it would be too far out of character for Amber. But a little color would be nice and surely won't be too dangerous.

When Reid appears surprised, I add hurriedly, "I don't think I'm tan enough at the moment to really pull off a sleeveless white dress."

He smiles, as if in understanding, and then pauses to reflect before he perks up. "Oh, I know. If you like the Greek look, we have an absolutely gorgeous option—but the color is bronze. Is that too much?"

"Let's try it. If it's too much, I can always go with this one."

"Or you can get both." He laughs as he adjusts a couple of the pins in the white gown. Then he and another assistant help me out of the first dress and then into the new one.

Once it's pinned, I stare at myself in the mirror again—this time with absolute delight. The bronze silk jersey fabric drapes gracefully over my shoulders in two thick straps that crisscross at the bodice in a low V-neck. The curves of my figure are emphasized by the clingy fabric and the wide, intricately beaded band that cinches just under my breasts. The drapes and softly pleated folds of fabric give it the same Grecian look I liked in the previous gown, but this one manages to look sensual and unique as well as sophisticated.

I clap my hands in excitement. "I love it!"

"It's divine. I wouldn't have thought about it for you, but it's stunning."

He and the other assistant fuss over me for a few minutes, as they admire my gorgeousness from every angle in the mirror. Then they take it off so it can be tailored for me in time for the ballet, and I change back into my pants and sweater.

I'm picking up my purse when Reid says in a teasing tone that indicates familiarity, "Mr. Worthing must have been a very good boy for you to agree to go to the ballet with him."

I blink in confusion. "What?"

Reid frowns, his brows drawing together. "I was just teasing. Everyone knows you despise the ballet and always refuse to go with him. I was just wondering at your change of heart."

I freeze, suddenly slammed with a wave of mortified heat. The flush moves from my cheeks to my neck and then down to the rest of my body.

I've blown it. I've *blown* it. I've given myself away. Without ever realizing I was doing so. Amber hates the ballet. I never knew that about her, but maybe it's a distaste she developed over the past several years. What the hell must William have thought when I agreed to go with him so easily? Why the hell had he invited me as if he assumed I wouldn't accept?

I mumble in a somewhat convincing tone, "He has been a very good boy." And I'm relieved when I'm able to leave the studio.

Had William been testing me? Does he suspect I'm not Amber?

No. It can't be. He's acted perfectly natural for the past few days and hasn't given any indication of suspicion or confusion. Not even the faint bewilderment I occasionally saw in him the first few weeks. If he knows I'm not Amber, he would have confronted me. Probably thrown me out. I can explain this fumble away. I can find a way to address it.

I just need to figure out how.

I've been to the ballet before, but I've never attended an exclusive, invitation-only, premiere performance like this one.

Everyone is dressed up. Everyone clearly understands this as an occasion. And everyone seems to be looking over at me and William—either openly or discreetly—as we enter the lobby and make our way up to our seats.

My logic tells me they aren't all looking at us, but it seems that way to me.

I feel absolutely gorgeous in my new gown. I've never felt so beautiful in my life. I'm wearing it with strappy bronze heels and a gold choker I found in Amber's jewelry box that used to be our grandmother's, set with a single dark brown gemstone that matches the beading in my dress. I've pulled my hair up into Amber's trademark chignon, but I can't keep a few loose strands from slipping out and framing my face. I made my eyes smoky with makeup and put on dark red lipstick, and I'm so ridiculously excited about my appearance that I might as well be a girl going to the prom.

William stared when I emerged from getting dressed. And he didn't say anything as we made our way down to the car, although he kept looking at me. Finally, when the driver pulled away from the curb, I was too uncomfortable under the intensity of his silent gaze and asked, "Well? Do I look all right?"

"Beautiful." He seemed to mean it. But he continued looking at me in that same way.

I'm not quite sure what it means. Probably admiration, but surely Amber has looked equally or even more beautiful than I do right now on multiple occasions. It's not like William isn't used to seeing her dressed up like this.

Maybe he's suspicious. Maybe he thinks the gown isn't right for Amber's style or he's still questioning my attending the ballet at all.

Either way, my stomach twists anxiously.

When we take our seats, I give him a slightly nervous smile. "Were you surprised I agreed to go with you tonight?"

He's looking at me thoughtfully, although the corner of his mouth is turned up in an almost smile. "You never have before."

"I know." I'm relieved to be able to pull out my prepared explanation for the incongruity. "I didn't want to make a big deal about it, but I'm trying to be better—like I said. And it just seems kind of selfish not to go when it's something you enjoy. So I thought I would give it a try. As a... as a gesture."

His smile widens. "Maybe you'll enjoy it."

"Maybe I will." I'm smiling back, relaxing now that William seems to have bought the explanation.

I do enjoy the ballet. I'm not any sort of dance connoisseur, but I love the beauty and the drama of the performance, as well as the skill, grace, and power of the performers. I'm mostly wrapped up in the dancing, but I occasionally get the feeling that William is watching me, so I occasionally dart a quick glance over to his face.

He's never looking at me.

During the intermission, we get up and stroll out to the upper lobby to get a glass of champagne and mingle. It's not long before we're surrounded by acquaintances, many people teasing Amber for finally attending the ballet and many others trying to touch base with William about a variety of business matters.

I follow the conversation as well as I can, but soon I'm getting disoriented from keeping up with so many people I don't know. I'm also starting to feel overly hot in the crowded, stuffy lobby space.

When I can't stand it anymore, I whisper to William that I'm going to get some air and walk out of the upper lobby and onto one of the terraces. There are a few other couples scattered about at the length of railing, but I move to an empty spot and stare out at the lights of the city.

It's too chilly to be outside with bare arms and a low neckline like this. I wore a thick wrap but left it at my seat. I don't care though. The brisk air is fresh and cool after the stuffiness of the lobby, and the quiet is a huge relief.

I breathe deeply and ignore the goose bumps that break out on my arms.

"It's too cold," William says, coming up behind me without warning. "You should go back inside."

I shake my head, smiling up at him. For some reason, the sight of his watchful brown eyes and handsome face makes me feel happy, familiar, secure. "I'm fine. It was too hot in there anyway."

Despite my words, my teeth chatter briefly as a shiver slices through me.

He rolls his eyes and takes off his black suit jacket, then

drapes it around my shoulders. It's warm and smells delicious—exactly like William. I burrow into it gratefully.

"Shouldn't you be schmoozing?" I glance over my shoulder at the crowded lobby with a teasing smile.

"I schmoozed enough."

I laugh, charmed by his characteristic dry humor. I can't remember ever finding anything more appealing than William's perfectly sober expression, broken only by the faintest twitch of his lips.

Instinctively, without thinking it through, I lean against his side, pleased when he puts one arm around me as we stand and look out at the view.

Not for the first time I wonder how Amber could be such a fool—to have a man like William and not want him.

Before I can second-guess the impulse, I hear myself asking, "Why are you doing this with me?"

I regret the question as soon as I voice it since it's too vague, too easily misinterpreted, and reveals too much about the dangerous way my emotions are drifting.

He grows very still. "Doing what?"

"This... relationship. Our arrangement. I know it's a practical arrangement, but it's really far to go for a business deal. So I was just..." I gulp. "Wondering."

He doesn't respond immediately. Turns his head to look down at my face.

"You don't have to answer if you don't want. I just can't help but wonder. I know I agreed to the arrangement too, but I have more obvious reasons than you. I don't... My family lost our money. It would be nice to get it back. But you... you don't need money. You already have a great reputation and a successful career. You don't need the Delacourte name that badly although I understand why it would be nice for you to get it. So why... why...?"

Again, he doesn't give an immediate answer. For just a moment, he looks almost trapped. Helpless.

I've never seen him look that way before.

"Can't you tell me?" I ask very softly.

He lets out a thick breath and looks away, staring out at the city like we were before. "It was... an escape."

"An escape from what?"

"From feeling like a failure."

"What?" I grab for his shirt, trying to pull him around to face me. "What are you talking about? You're the farthest thing from a failure I've ever seen."

"Thanks for that. But the feeling isn't rational. It's planted deep. My dad and my uncle both made it clear I wasn't likely to live up to their expectations. That truth was hammered home all my life. My dad wasn't violent the way Arthur's father sometimes was, but he was... so cold. Ruthless. I think he was trying to forge me into someone stronger because he always thought I was too weak and sensitive. But it proved to me over and over again that I'd never measure up."

I'm horrified by this confession, by what it says about

his family and background. "That's despicable. I can't believe they did that to you. Have you ever... talked through what they did to you? With a professional, I mean."

"I've been to therapy. Starting in college and for years afterward. I'm convinced it's the only reason I'm basically functional now. But then I got absorbed in work and found myself channeling all that pain into professional success. When I first approached you and you suggested the arrangement, I knew it wasn't rational. I knew it was the voices of my dad and uncle still speaking to me from the grave. But I did it anyway. They could never get the Delacourtes on board, so if I could... If I could, it would prove something. Vindicate me."

He laughs softly, slightly bitter. "I've also always been expected to marry and have children, especially when it became clear that Arthur was going to shirk that responsibility. After all, we need more Worthing heirs to pass on all our hang-ups and neuroses to. So a loveless marriage without children seemed like appropriate vengeance. Petty, but sadly true."

I'm both intrigued and touched by his intimate revelation. I never dreamed I'd hear something so deep and real from him. It sits in my chest like a weight. I reach out to rub his back softly.

"I never would have pursued it," he adds, glancing over. "I never would have thought of it myself. But then the idea was... dropped in my lap, and it felt like fate to me."

The fake marriage was clearly Amber's idea. She made it happen and then ran away.

I really wish I could shake her.

William doesn't need anyone else to hurt him. He's already had a lifetime of it.

We stand in silence for a long minute, wrapped up in our own thoughts. I feel closer to him right now than I've ever felt to anyone since Amber and I were close as kids.

I shouldn't. It's stupid and dangerous and wrong to feel this way about a man who is supposed to be with my sister.

But I do anyway.

"What about you?" His questions break into my reverie.

"What about me?"

"Is it just the money? Is that the only reason you're with me?"

My breath hitches as my eyes fly to his face. He's looking at me now, something questioning, almost soft in his eyes.

I swallow hard. I don't want to lie—it feels utterly wrong to do so at this moment—but I also have to frame an answer that works for Amber. "It's not just the money." I lower my eyes. "It's so many things. At first I was... trapped. I couldn't see any other choice. So I... I used you. I didn't want to, but I did. But there's more to it than that. You're

William Worthing—handsome, powerful, brilliant, sexy as hell. Who wouldn't want to be with that man?"

I don't dare to look up at him. Just press on. "But... but that man isn't really a match for me. Not really. And it was when I could see the man beneath the image. The real man. Who isn't that much different from me. That's when I knew. That's who I want to be with."

It's true. It's foolishly, painfully true. And I have to swallow over the ache of knowledge that I've fallen for the man I'm deceiving, the man who still believes he's with my sister.

Before I can fully process the realization, William puts a hand on my face and tilts it up again. I have the brief consciousness of his expression being hot, deep, overwhelming, before he leans down to kiss me.

And then I'm not aware of anything but a rush of pleasure, feeling, and excitement. My arms wind around his neck eagerly as I open to the advance of his tongue. We kiss deeply, passionately, and I moan into his mouth helplessly as he presses my body against his. He's hot and hard and strong and hungry, and I want to feel him completely.

When our lips break apart at last, I gasp desperately and let my head fall back as his mouth trails down my jaw and throat. "Oh God, William." My body tightens with desire even as a blur of feeling makes my eyes glaze over. I claw at his shoulders and back, trying to pull him even closer to me.

His hands slip under the jacket he gave me to wear and brush over my breasts before they slide down my ribs and waist to cup my bottom over my slinky dress. "Fuck," he grits out, his voice muffled by my lips, which he's claimed again. "I want you so much."

I want him too. And I'm not sure how I'm going to keep resisting what I want so much. Maybe if—when—he says Amber's name, I'll come back to my senses and remember how wrong this is.

But he doesn't say Amber's name. He doesn't say anything as he kisses me deeply again.

It feels like we're alone, but we aren't. We're on a public terrace in view of who knows how many socialites and bigwigs. We really shouldn't be embracing so shamelessly.

I'm almost relieved when a voice over the intercom announces that the second half of the ballet is about to begin.

I break away from William with a groan. He groans too, his eyes glazed with heated intensity and perspiration visible on his forehead. He rubs at his face, obviously trying to pull it together.

"We should wait on this," I manage to say, praying that by the time the ballet is over I can have regained my sense of perspective and find the resolve to have a migraine. "Until a more propitious time."

"We can always leave now." His voice is thick but

sounding more like himself. "And reach the more propitious time sooner."

I chuckle, despite myself, at his cleverness. "I'm enjoying the ballet more than I thought. Let's go back in."

William agrees without objection, and we return to our seats just as the lights are dimming.

The second half of the ballet is as impressive as the first, but I have a hard time concentrating.

I have a hard time doing anything but thinking about William—about how he will never truly be mine.

7

ON THE FOLLOWING THURSDAY, I CHECK MY ROASTED chicken and potatoes in the oven, pleased to see they look perfectly done and absolutely delicious.

I've always generally enjoyed cooking, but I've never cooked as much as I have lately. But Amber's life is so leisurely and decadent that I have to find goals to focus on and accomplish wherever I can. Cooking a variety of dishes for dinner—generally fairly simple since I use whatever Greta has stocked for the week—is one of the things I can do.

Since dinner is almost ready, I leave the kitchen and walk down the hallway. I mentioned to William that I'm making dinner, and although he gave me a murmured, indefinite answer, I assumed he would join me.

Overall, he's been a little standoffish since the ballet

last week, but he's fallen into the habit of eating dinner with me when he's home at a reasonable time.

His reticence the past several days has been almost a relief since it's now obvious I'm getting in too deep with him and there are no possible scenarios where I won't end up getting hurt at the end of this. I can't live this lie forever. Either William will find out who I am and throw me out. Or Amber will decide she wants her life back and throw me out. Or Detective Curtis will keep snooping around and the truth will come out, in which case William will throw me out.

Or Montaigne will kill me.

I've spent hours trying to make contingency plans, but I haven't come up with anything that will solve the basic problem of my life.

The ironic thing is I've barely thought about Montaigne for weeks now. I've been safe here as a different person, protected by all of William's resources. I haven't felt so safe since I left home, and despite all the lingering anxiety, I'm not sure I've ever been so happy in my life.

Ludicrous. Tragic. But true.

I pause in the hallway as I approach William's home office. I must have left the door halfway open after I stopped in earlier to mention dinner. I wonder if William is even aware of its being opened since the door is always closed. I hear his voice and realize he's on the phone. Without thinking, I listen to what he's saying.

"How was she able to access the account?" William is asking, his voice muffled from inside the study. He doesn't sound happy at all.

After a moment of silence, during which the other person on the call must be speaking, William continues, "That's unacceptable. So I'm to understand, if we hadn't been intentionally looking for it, she would have been able to withdraw funds from that account without our being aware of it?"

My eyes widen. Evidently someone is trying to steal from William. An employee, most likely. I'm sure it happens often enough in business settings, but what a difficult and stressful situation to deal with.

"I don't need excuses," he says, after another pause. "Address the negligence in security immediately."

In response to what must be a question from the person he's talking to, William responds, "No. Give her access to the funds for now so we can find out what she's planning and if anyone else is involved. Have you found out any more information about my... other situation?"

The response must have been a long one since the silence goes on for a few minutes. Finally William says, "Good. So you haven't found signs of... malicious intent?"

Whatever the answer is must satisfy him since William says, "Good, thank you. Keep investigating." Then he hangs up the phone.

I freeze in the hallway, torn between options. William

sounds so unhappy about his employee's betrayal of him that part of me wants to go comfort him and another part of me wants to run away and hide.

I can't do either, however. I'm not supposed to have heard that private conversation, and dinner is ready. I take a few deep breaths, square my shoulders, and make my way to the partly open office door.

I'm raising a hand to knock when I catch a glimpse of William inside the room. He's seated at his computer, so he's not directly facing the door. His head is lowered into his hand, and his shoulders are hunched.

He looks exhausted. Battered. Defeated.

The sight of him makes my chest ache.

I manage to resist the urge to run over and comfort him. Instead, I knock briskly on the door.

He straightens with a jerk and cuts his eyes over to where I'm standing in the doorway. His expression is immediately guarded. "Yes?"

I swallow, irrationally hurt by his tone. "Sorry to bother you. Dinner is ready if you're hungry."

William pauses for a moment, then shakes his head. "I'm pretty busy here. I'll just get something later."

I open my mouth to argue but then stop myself. I don't have the right to insist that he joins me. He's obviously gotten some bad news this evening, and he isn't in a social mood. I can hardly blame him for wanting to be alone.

No matter how much I might want to do so, William isn't mine to take care of.

"All right." I manage a fairly convincing smile. "There will be plenty of leftovers if you want any later."

I feel heavy and depressed as I return to the kitchen. I pull the chicken and potatoes out of the oven and plate some up for myself. I eat it with a glass of wine at the bar in the kitchen. It's really good, but I don't enjoy it as much as I normally would.

I should just leave. I can't keep lying to William like this. It isn't fair to him, and it's too emotionally dangerous for me. Tomorrow I can go out shopping and sneak away from the driver. Catch a bus to somewhere else.

The only money I have access to doesn't belong to me, and there's no way I'm going to steal any of William's money. But I could take a few pieces of my mom's jewelry to sell. Half of it is mine by rights.

Maybe it will be enough to set up a new life. A new identity. Maybe Montaigne won't find me this time.

It's a risk. A real risk. But it's the right thing to do.

I can't stop thinking about William alone in his study —hungry and discouraged. So, when I finish eating, I make up another plate of chicken, potatoes, and rolls. I pour a glass of wine and get the napkin and silverware together. Then carry everything to William's study.

The door is closed all the way, but I summon my courage and knock after rejuggling the plate and glass in my hands. There isn't a response. After a minute, I knock again. "William?"

"Come in." His tone isn't promising.

I open the door anyway. If I'm going to leave tomorrow, it won't matter if he gets annoyed with me tonight. "I brought you some dinner. It won't be as good warmed up later."

He stares for a moment, looking vaguely surprised. But then his face softens slightly. "Thanks."

I carry the meal over to his desk and set it down on the credenza near his chair. Then I look down at his handsome, guarded face. He opened up to me at the ballet last weekend, but that doesn't mean he's entirely remade. He'll always be a difficult man—wounded and closed off and resisting any sort of vulnerability.

It doesn't matter anymore. I'm leaving tomorrow.

"Thanks," William says again, looking from my face to the food. "It looks good."

"It turned out okay." I want to say something else. Anything else.

Tell him thank you. I'm so sorry. Goodbye.

That I might have accidentally fallen in love with him.

My chest hurts so much I can barely breathe. But I swallow over the strangling lump and give him a little nod. "Okay. Don't work too hard."

Then I leave. He doesn't stop me.

I clean my mess in the kitchen and go to the media

room to read on the couch. When I can't focus on the words for more than five minutes at a time, I give up. Take a long bath and go to bed.

I doze off eventually, in spite the flurry of thoughts and emotions in my head. But I don't sleep deeply and wake up immediately when William comes into the bedroom after midnight.

I turned off the lights earlier, so I watch him covertly in the darkness of the room as he starts to undress and then goes into the bathroom. I hear the shower running for a long time. Then he finally comes back out.

I can see before he turns off the bathroom light that he's wearing nothing but a pair of black boxers, which is what he normally wears to sleep. And I feel the bed shift as he gets under the covers beside me.

It feels like he's looking at me in the dark.

"Are you okay?" I ask hoarsely, surprising myself by speaking. I'm groggy and disoriented, and my chest still aches intensely.

I want to cry, but I can't. For so many reasons.

"Yes."

I don't believe him.

"Are *you* all right?" he asks in the dark after a moment.

"No." It sounds like he really cares.

"Come here." He reaches out to pull me against him.

I scoot over, letting him wrap his arms around me as I press the length of my body against his. He feels tense and strangely needy, and I hug him as tightly as I can. He smells like William—like he's had a long, hard day—and the familiar fragrance makes my heart hurt even more.

We don't say anything, so I don't have to lie. We hold each other for a long time. When I finally feel William's body start to relax, I realize that I'm relaxing too. Despite myself, I'm comforted, and I think he must feel that way too.

Eventually I fall asleep, my body still fitting snuggly against his.

It can likely be explained by the fact that I've been living for almost two months with a man I'm increasingly attracted to without having any outlet for that attraction. And also by the fact that I've been sleeping pressed up against him all night. But, for whatever reason, I dream about sex.

It's a vague, abstract dream—with no storyline or clear details. But it's deeply erotic, and the sensation of bodies, of urgency, of intensifying need grows stronger and stronger as the dream progresses.

The feelings are so intense I'm not even conscious of waking up just before dawn. My body has reacted to the carnality of the dream, and my hips are moving in response to that urgency.

My skin is flushed. My nipples tight and aching. The pressure between my legs is so intense I can't keep from moaning. I'm grinding myself against the hard, hot man beside me, trying to ease some of the torturous physical need.

William. The man is William. And he's lean and strong and deliciously warm. His body is as tense as mine, and one of his arms is wrapped around me.

I moan again as I rub my groin against his thigh, and my hand, without volition, strays down his body until I find the bulge of his erection in his boxers. I squeeze there, panting against his chest as he groans thickly in response.

He must wake up just then since his body gives a little jerk, and then he rolls over on top of me, fumbling through a series of kisses until he finds my mouth.

It's exactly what I want—what I need—so I kiss him back, squirming shamelessly beneath the delicious press of his body.

As we kiss, William pushes up my little camisole, baring my breasts. Then he lowers his head until he can take one nipple in his mouth.

I cry out uninhibitedly at the sharp tug of pleasure. As he continues to suckle, I arch up into the sensations and try to wrap one of my legs around his hips. I can't stop moaning, my voice too loud, too enthusiastic. I can't seem to think. Can't possibly control myself.

I want this—him—so much.

After a minute, the exquisite torment of his mouth on my breast is too much. I claw at his shoulders and beg him to stop. We both fumble with our clothes until we've gotten them off. Then he rolls back on top of me, parting my legs and settling there until he's lined himself up at my entrance.

His face is above mine again, only a few inches away, and we are panting with equal urgency.

"Please, please, William," I gasp when he hesitates, the tip of his erection teasing me.

"You want me?" His voice is so thick it's almost unrecognizable.

"Yeah, yeah, I want you so much." I lift my pelvis, desperate to feel him inside me.

"For real."

"Oh God, yes. Please."

"I want *you*, sweetheart. Fuck, I want you too." Then, at last, he slides himself home.

I gasp loudly as he enters me, the pressure deliciously tight. It's been a long time since I've had sex, and this feels as right as anything ever has.

William freezes, holding himself above me. My eyes are blurry from sleep and desire, but I can dimly see his features twisting with pleasure and effort. "Oh fuck, you feel so good."

I can't wait any longer. I start to ride him enthusiastically from below, making childish little bursts of sounds as the friction satisfies my deepest ache.

William gives a muffled groan and then begins to thrust. His motion is fast, hard, clumsy, just as out of control as mine.

I drag my nails down his back, my gasps turning into sobs as an orgasm tightens. William is riding me hard, shaking the bed so vigorously that the headboard bangs against the wall. He's huffing out rhythmic, wordless sounds that are hot and primitive and exactly what I want to hear.

I arch up off the bed as my climax breaks, crying out loudly as the intense pleasure moves through me. As my channel clamps down around his shaft, William loses it too. He jerks through a series of clumsy thrusts as his face transforms with transparent pleasure. Then he's coming inside me, letting out a relieved exclamation that's almost as loud as mine.

The spasms last a long time, but eventually we've worked through them with lingering moans and little jerks of our hips. He collapses on top of me at last, and I hold him as tightly as I can, relishing the release of so much tension and the deeper pleasure of having given him what he needs.

But, with the physical urgency finally gone, the last groggy haze of sleep lifts. William must have been half-asleep in our lovemaking too, or he wouldn't have let go so quickly and so completely.

I never should have done this.

He's heavy and hot and relaxed on top of me, his face buried in the hollow of my neck. He's pressing clumsy kisses against my skin and murmuring out something I can't quite understand.

It sounds almost like my name. My real name. Jade.

But that's ridiculous. Nothing more than wishful thinking.

William thinks he just had sex with Amber. Not me. And this is wrong—utterly wrong—in so many ways.

A torrent of emotion overtakes me before I can stop it, and I push at William's shoulders almost desperately. I have just enough sense remaining to mumble out an excuse. "Sorry. You're kind of heavy, and I need to go to the bathroom."

He finally rolls off with a groan, and I scramble up and run into the bathroom.

I sit down on the edge of the tub and cry, smothering the sound as much as I can.

After a few minutes, there's a tap on the bathroom door. "You okay?" William asks from the hall, sounding controlled and natural.

"Yeah," I reply, managing to force down the sobs. "I'm going to take a shower, if that's all right."

"Okay."

I turn the water in the shower on hot and stand under it for a long time, releasing my emotions until I've finally cried myself out.

It's awful. The whole thing is awful. I never should have had sex with him. I never should have fallen for him. I never should have lied to him in the first place. But I can't change it now. I can't take any of it back.

I just have to leave.

I can't take advantage of William any more than I already have.

So I turn off the shower, dry off, peek out at the bedroom and am relieved that it's empty. It's almost six now, so he's probably pulled on some clothes and gone to work in his home office.

I get dressed in a pair of jeans I find at the back of Amber's closet and a thin gray sweater. I put a few pieces of my mom's jewelry into a bag. Nothing else here is mine, so I don't take it.

I peer out into the hall and see that William's office door is shut.

It's safe then. He's already absorbed in business. That's what he does. He works to hide from pain.

Me, I just run away.

I hurry toward the entryway and slide on my shoes, which I left there after I came in yesterday.

I walk out, explaining to the doorman that I'm taking a stroll and don't need the car.

It's as easy as that. I walk out of the apartment, out of the building, out of William's life for good.

It hurts as much as anything ever has, but I do it anyway.

The morning is brisk and cool, and—even though it's just after six o'clock—the sidewalks and streets aren't empty. People are already out and about, beginning their days.

It's not the end for them like it is for me.

I walk a few blocks toward where the closest metro station is, but when I get there I can't go down. I should. I need to take the metro to a reputable jeweler who will buy my mom's pieces for cash. I won't get anywhere close to what the items in my bag are worth, but I'll get a lot more than I would from a pawnshop.

Cash in hand, I can take another metro to the big bus hub outside the city and from there go... somewhere. Preferably not a big city. A smaller area with a lower cost of living.

Anywhere other than here.

But I can't do it. Make that final step. It's not simply terrifying—being on my own again, no protection, at the mercy of a stalker who will never quit. Without any sort of plan for taking care of myself.

It's also heartbreaking.

I'll never see William again.

My legs won't support me so I find an empty bench at

the small park across the street and sit down. I'm too numb to cry anymore, so I sit in a daze for several minutes, willing myself to get up and do what I know I need to do.

Eventually a flurry of activity across the street distracts me. A man is running toward the metro station, fast enough to draw attention. He's wearing nothing but a pair of sweats, a T-shirt, and a pair of slippers.

William.

My heart flutters, but the rest of me is too numb to react. Before he turns toward the stairs into the station, something prompts him to glance around. His eyes find me where I'm sitting on the bench.

He's too far away for me to read his expression, but he changes course immediately. Slows down and crosses the street. He's breathing heavily but doesn't say anything when he reaches me.

He sits down beside me.

This is my fault. I could have been away by now—on an entirely new course for my life. I could have already left this huge, tragic mess behind me and started over.

Instead, I need an excuse for leaving the apartment without a word. William ran after me. He clearly knows something is wrong.

"I wanted some air," I say at last, the slightest wobble in my tone.

He turns his head. His skin is flushed, and his hair is messy. He hasn't shaved or showered yet this morning and went to bed with his hair damp last night. His breath is still coming out in fast pants.

He must have really been booking it.

"Did you?" he asks hoarsely.

"Did you think I freaked out?"

"Yes." He says the words on a bitterly amused huff. "That's what I thought."

"I'm sorry. I shouldn't have left like that. I just needed... I wanted..." I have no idea how to finish the sentence because everything I truly want is sitting on the bench beside me right now. What I was doing earlier wasn't what I wanted. It was a last gasp of guilt and confusion.

He's thinking. I can see it on his face. His brain is working through some sort of complex problem with his typical sharp intelligence. He finally says softly, "I know neither of us intended to have sex earlier. I should have stopped to clear up the ambiguity, but I wasn't... I wasn't awake enough to make good decisions. I am sorry about that. If it's bothering you, if it's not what you want, we can agree not to do it again. I won't slip up again."

"No, William, don't take it all on you. I'm just as much at fault. I wasn't fully awake either, but I did want..." I pause to clear my throat. "I wanted it. I did. Things for me are just... really messy."

He's quiet again for a full minute, staring at a spot in front of him, thinking hard. "If they're too messy," he says at last. "If it's too much for you, if you want to leave, you can. I won't stop you. I can help you."

The offer is so kindhearted and so reluctant at the same time, I make a helpless whimper. This is my chance. He's set me up for it perfectly. I could tell him the truth and explain how I need a new identity. He has the resources to get me one that Montaigne will never discover.

But he's being a decent guy and letting Amber out of her contract with him. He's not offering to save the woman who lied her way into his house and his bed.

And, besides, the crux of the matter still hasn't changed.

I simply don't want to leave.

"That's not what I want," I tell him, rubbing my face and trying to figure out what's the best thing to do. "I just needed... some air."

"Okay."

We sit some more in silence. His breathing has finally slowed, but I can still hear him inhale and exhale. It almost feels like I can hear the gears of his mind working.

Mine is mostly a blank.

"The truth is," William says at last, "things are messy for me too."

"I know they are."

He's going to end it now. I know it for sure. And I hate it

—hate it—even knowing it will make my decisions from here on out so much simpler.

"So what if we..." He shifts his position on the bench so he's halfway facing me. "What if we were to—for now—put the mess behind us?"

"What?" My eyes widen. My lips part. This isn't at all what I expected, and I have no idea where he's going with it.

"What if we press pause on the mess for a while? So we can take the time to see what this thing actually is." He gestures with his hand between the two of us, indicating the nature of *this thing*. "Then later, if we decide it's worth it, we can dig into the mess and try to sort it out."

It's like a dream. Like the answer to a prayer. Like a wish come to life. Putting off everything that's tearing me up for a while and having a safe space to be with William.

It shouldn't have been possible, but he's making it so.

"You'd be okay..." I'm speaking in breathless gasps, so I have to start again. "You want that?"

"Honestly, I'm not remotely sure what I want. I guarantee I'm as confused as you are. But I do know this." He clears his throat. "I don't want you to leave."

"I don't want to leave either," I say in almost a whisper.

"Then don't. Sweetheart, please don't leave me."

My face twists with a surge of emotion, but I don't break into tears. I give him a shaky smile. "Okay. I won't."

He stands up with a slight wince, as if he's stiff or sore. Then he reaches his arm out, offering me his hand.

I take it, letting him help me to my feet.

He holds my hand as we walk back toward our building. Even as we maneuver around other pedestrians on the sidewalk, he doesn't let it go.

When we get back to the apartment, I have no idea what to do.

It's six thirty on a Friday morning, but it feels like I've lived several lifetimes in the past twelve hours.

William appears equally restless and bemused. We stand in the entryway, looking at each other.

"I guess you'll probably need to take a shower and be heading to work." I lift my voice slightly at the end to make it a question.

"Yeah. I should." He still doesn't move.

"Unless you want to take the day off?"

He huffs softly, his eyes softening. "I do want that. But I've got meetings stacked on top of each other starting at ten."

"Oh. Ugh."

"Yeah."

"Well, you've got plenty of time to shower and dress and get to work if your first meeting doesn't start until ten.

Maybe you can come home at a reasonable time tonight and we can... we can hang out?"

He smiles. "Yes. We can definitely hang out this evening."

I perk up at the promise in his tone. "Okay then. If you don't think me too lazy, I might go back to bed for a couple of hours."

"Sounds like a very good plan to me."

I change back into pajamas and climb into bed while he takes a shower. I'm still awake, tired and flustered and ridiculously giddy, when he comes out into the bedroom wearing nothing but a towel.

I smile at him from my pillow, hoping my hair isn't too embarrassing.

"You shouldn't look like that when I'm supposed to be getting ready for work," he says.

"Look like what?"

"Like temptation personified, luring me back into bed."

I suck in a quick breath, suddenly hot. "I wasn't trying to seduce you!"

"I know you weren't. But you're still almost impossible to resist."

Now that sex has entered the air, I can't think of anything else. I'm immediately excited, arousal clenching hard between my legs. I glance over at the clock. "Well, you still have some time, if you don't want to resist that temptation."

He smiles with a leisurely heat that makes me gulp. "You want it too?"

"I definitely want it."

He's moved to the bed now, his body firm and lean and fit and masculine. I can see the shape of a partial erection beneath his towel. "Good. Because I'd like to show you what I can do when I'm not half-asleep."

"I was pretty happy with what you could do when you were half-asleep."

He chuckles and drops his towel. "I think we can do even better this time."

When he climbs into the bed with me, he's as good as his word, taking a long time to kiss and caress me until I'm desperately turned on, squirming and gasping and making silly mewing sounds that I've never heard myself make before.

Finally, I assume he's ready to get to the main event, but he takes another detour, kissing his way down my body until he's nuzzling at my groin. I have to reach up and grab the headboard when he pulls my thighs apart and starts to work on me with his tongue and lips and face.

He makes me come twice before he's done, and he's smiling in pleased pride when he straightens up.

I giggle, my body warm and soft and relaxed from my orgasms. "You shouldn't look so smug."

"Oh yes, I should."

"Fine. You're really good at that. Thank you."

"You don't have to thank me. It was the hottest thing ever. Do you want me to use a condom? We didn't earlier, so I hope that wasn't a—"

"It's okay. I'm on birth control." Amber was, and I've been taking her pills to sustain the ruse. "I think we'll be fine without a condom, unless you'd rather use one."

He shakes his head and moves over me so he can kiss me slow and soft. Then he bends my legs and guides himself inside me, the tight penetration causing both of us to groan.

I'm a little sore from the sex we had a couple of hours ago, but not enough to matter. I hold on to his ass as he starts to pump, loving that I'm allowed to do so.

He takes me like that for several minutes. I have a number of small, fluttery climaxes and thoroughly enjoy it. Then he repositions onto his knees and raises my bottom, entering me again. He's finally losing his control. His motion becomes faster and harder.

Both of us are grunting and panting as we build momentum, until I'm suddenly crying out loudly as a more powerful orgasm hits me unexpectedly. I shake and gasp and whimper as he keeps fucking me through it, and I haven't yet come down when he lets go too.

He lies on top of me for a long time afterward as the last shudders of pleasure fade and our bodies relax. He occasionally presses a kiss against the crook of my neck.

He's not much of a talker in bed, but he doesn't have to be.

I know how much he needed this and how much he enjoyed it. Just as much as I did.

I don't think I've ever felt closer to anyone else in my life.

A small flicker of a thought reminds me that he doesn't even know my real name, but we've pressed pause on the mess.

We've pressed pause.

So I let the thought slip out of my mind.

8

_____

THE NEXT TWO WEEKS ARE GOOD.

Really good.

Probably the best in my life.

I try not to think too deeply about what this means or what might happen after our pause-the-mess period is over.

If I brood on it too much, I won't be able to enjoy the time I've been given. Instead of brooding, I wake up with William every morning, spend my days making jewelry with an occasional appointment or coffee date with Haley, and hang out with William in the evenings, talking, going for walks, eating dinners, and having a lot of sex.

I never knew life could be so good.

It's another Friday morning when I wake up as soon as William rolls away from me and sits up. I usually awaken when he does. At first, because I was so anxious, I had to be on guard against anything that might happen and now because I've become attuned to his presence. Usually I give him a mumbled greeting and go back to sleep, but today is different.

I'm fully awake in about ten seconds. I open my eyes and lift my head. "Hey."

William is sitting on the edge of the bed. He's wearing nothing but his boxers, and his hair is sticking out in all directions. "Hey." He turns his head and gives me a quiet smile.

It feels like there's a string tied to my heart extending all the way over to him. It's being tugged right now. I can feel it in my chest.

I scoot over so I can sit next to him. "You okay?"

"Yeah."

"Big day."

He slants me a quick look. Then nods. "It is."

Today they sign the final contracts on the restructuring of the Worthing companies and holdings. Everything he's been working toward will finally come to fruition.

I reach over and take his hand, holding it in my lap with both of mine. "Are you excited? Nervous?"

"Wired. And also exhausted. If it's possible to be both at the same time."

I lean my head against his shoulder, stroking his palm with both my thumbs. "It's definitely possible. But it will be great. You're going to do great."

"I hope so."

"Do you really think you won't?"

He doesn't answer immediately. He adjusts the clasp of our hands so he can bring one of mine up to his mouth and press a kiss on the knuckles.

"William, you're brilliant and focused and committed and you work so hard. How can you not do a good job?"

He smiles. "Thank you for that."

"I'm not saying anything other than the truth. You'll see. I'm sure your cousin did a fine job, but he was pulled in a zillion directions and he never even wanted all that responsibility. You do want it. These specific companies are going to have your full attention, and heading them up is exactly what you want to do. You're going to blow everyone away."

He's smiling again, softer and warmer this time. "I'm going to do my best."

"That's all you have to do. But you're allowed to be excited. You've worked really hard for this."

"I have."

I wrap both arms around him and squeeze him in a long hug. He doesn't say anything else, but he doesn't have to. I can feel his response in his nakedly needy grip on me.

Two months ago, I never dreamed William Worthing might need me for real. For anything.

But he does.

He *does*.

That evening, we have dinner with Arthur Worthing and his girlfriend, Scarlett, to celebrate the completed restructuring.

Arthur is William's oldest cousin and about ten years older than him. Because of this, they were never really close, but he's talked about him being a good guy. I honestly have no idea what to expect, but I guess I imagined a slightly older version of William.

Arthur Worthing is nothing like William. He's got long hair that reaches his shoulders—brown threaded with gray. Although he's got it pulled back in a loose, low ponytail, it still comes across as rather rumpled. He has strong, roughly attractive features and a large scar slashing down one side of his face. His suit is well tailored but not as sleekly professional as William's.

Other than the exact same brown eyes, I'd never know they were related.

His girlfriend is much younger than him—probably my age—and quietly pretty with brown hair and amber eyes. She comes across as thoughtful and intelligent, and she has a lovely, soft, lyrical voice. She's not one of those highly social extroverts, but she's easy to talk to.

I like her immediately. When I see her giving me a quick, automatic assessment, I really hope she doesn't assume I'm a wannabe trophy wife, only interested in obtaining a rich husband.

That was mostly true of my sister, but it's not at all true of me.

I'm wearing Amber's stylish clothes and accessories, which are much more fashion-conscious than Scarlett's. She has a graduate degree and a career working with rare books, while right now I do nothing but fiddle with jewelry and spend a lot of money.

It suddenly bothers me that this other woman might think I'm looking for an easy lifestyle. That I don't want William for real—for who he is.

We go through introductions and preliminaries at the bar until the host comes over to tell us our table is ready. As we're walking over, William puts a hand on the back of my neck and slows me down, leaning over to murmur, "What's wrong?"

I blink up at him in surprise. "What do you mean?"

"Something is bothering you. Don't you like them?"

"Oh yes. Of course I do. They both seem great."

"Then what's going on?" His eyes search my face with unnerving scrutiny.

I sigh. Part of me still wants to deflect, but I tell him the truth anyway. "It's nothing big. Just feeling like an empty-headed loser surrounded by such smart, successful people."

"What the hell?" he mutters. He's stopped walking now. Turns me toward him so he can see me fully.

"It's silly and irrational. It just feels like I haven't accomplished anything. And I don't want... anyone to think I'm just after a rich husband."

He's frowning as he gazes down at me, but the resonance shifts from disapproval to consideration. "Why would anyone think that about you?"

I almost giggle. "Oh my God, William. I guarantee you that's what two-thirds of people who meet us assume. You fund my lifestyle of shopping and salon appointments, and I'm a glittery accessory in your life. It's fine." With a sigh, I remember that William believes I'm Amber. His agreement with Amber was a financially driven arrangement. Openly so. "Actually, it's true."

"It is not true." He scowls. "You are not an accessory. Don't you dare objectify yourself that way."

He's so defensive—defensive of me—that my chest aches. My face twists briefly. "Thank you."

He leans down to kiss me quickly. Then he puts a hand on my back and guides me over to catch up with Arthur and Scarlett at our table.

I shake off my insecurities so I can be a good conversationalist. William is reserved by nature, and he doesn't talk easily in social situations except for the kind of empty niceties that are typical of cocktail parties. Tonight he's quieter than normal, so I make extra effort to maintain pleasant interaction. Arthur is clearly as reserved as William, but he's more relaxed. Although Scarlett and I are the primary talkers, Arthur smiles a lot and asks some interested questions.

We talk about Scarlett's work and about the future of the Worthing holdings and how Scarlett had a serious head injury and ended up with amnesia that took her memory of six whole months of her life.

The story is fascinating and heart-wrenching, and I ask a lot of follow-up questions because I'm so invested in it. So dinner passes quickly. After we order dessert, Scarlett must decide she's talked enough about herself. She changes to subject to ask about me.

I have to tell her I never went to college and never had a job. The job thing isn't true about me, but it is true about Amber and that's who I'm supposed to be.

Before Scarlett can reply, William cuts in. "She makes amazing jewelry. Show them your bracelet."

He hasn't been talking a lot, so I'm startled and stare at him for a minute before I can respond. Flushing slightly, I unlatch the bracelet on my wrist and pass it over to Scarlett. "It's nothing special."

Scarlett appears genuinely delighted as she looks down at the bracelet. It's a delicate gold chain of sculpted links and pretty, inexpensive sapphires.

I'm proud of it. It's one of my favorite pieces I've made

recently. But now I'm the center of attention, and I don't know what to do with it.

"It's beautiful!" Scarlett's eyes are big and sincere. "You actually made this?"

"Yeah. It's in the family. Delacourte. You know? We all learn the skills."

She admires it for a long time, clearly awed, and then passes it over to Arthur.

He studies it closely. "This is remarkable." His eyes lift to my face. "This is more than skill. It's art."

I flush deeper, pleased and gratified and self-conscious. "Thanks." I bite off the impulse to say it's not that good.

The fact is the bracelet is good. Better than good. And I made it.

Arthur gives the bracelet to William, who looks at it for a minute, turning it in his hand, before he passes it back to me.

As I latch it back on my wrist, I slant a look over at William. He's watching me, his eyes softer than usual. He's the one who brought the bracelet to attention. He wanted to make sure I don't believe I'm an empty-headed loser.

He's proud of me.

Genuinely.

And he wants other people to see what I can do too.

"Told you," he murmured.

I half giggle and half sob—embarrassed by a surge of emotion. I give him a teasing nudge with my elbow, and he reaches out to gently stroke the top of my hand with his fingertips.

Fortunately, our desserts come just then so the conversation shifts to something more casual.

After we finish eating, Scarlett and I excuse ourselves to the restroom.

Because I feel comfortable with her now, I take that opportunity to ask her about how she met and fell in love with Arthur. They're not a predictable couple, and I'm fascinated with how they even met to begin with.

She answers easily, rather sheepishly. He was a friend of her father's and gave her a job after her father died. The six months she lost to amnesia were the months when she fell in love with Arthur, so she ended up falling in love with him twice.

I'm even more intrigued by their love story, and I would have asked more questions had she not turned the conversation back to me as we're washing our hands.

She says, "So tell me about you and William."

I should have expected the question, but I'm put on the spot anyway. "It's... complicated."

"In what way?"

I throw away my paper towel and stare at myself in the mirror. "I'm not sure if I can explain it."

"Try."

"I'm..." What the hell can I say? I want to be friends with this woman, so I don't want to lie, but I can hardly tell her the whole truth. I haven't even told William. "It started kind of... superficially between us."

This doesn't appear to surprise her. She nods.

I blurt out, "But now I'm crazy about him."

"What's wrong with that? He clearly isn't averse to you either."

"You think so?" I probably sound too needy, but I really want to hear this. I crave it like a drug.

"Of course. He's hard to read, but there's definitely something there. Have you not talked about it?"

"Uh, yeah. Kind of. But everything isn't sorted out. And..." I have to stifle a surge of emotion as I think about the reality of my situation.

No matter how much I want William, he wants Amber instead.

I manage to complete my reply. "It's hard not to believe he wants someone other than me."

"I don't believe that, but if you're worried about it, then you need to talk to him again. *Kind of* talking isn't enough."

She's right. Of course she's right. But who wants to hear that sort of truth when it means you finally have to take an incredibly frightening step.

Scarlett goes on, "I'm not saying it will be easy. But you won't get what you need unless you take it."

I manage a little nod and then take a deep breath, trying to compose myself. "Sorry to dump that on you."

"You didn't dump anything. I asked. If you want to talk

more, give me a call. The truth is, I can use some more friends."

It feels like I've been given a gift. "Me too."

We linger for a long time at dinner, so it's late when William's driver finally picks us up to take us home.

Other than his comments about my jewelry and some basic courteous responses, William hasn't said much. And he's quieter than ever as we climb into the back of the car.

When I ask him how he's feeling, he tells me he's fine, so I don't push it. I lean against him as we sit together in the back seat, and eventually he puts an arm around me. I hear him sigh. Then his body starts to relax.

It's slow going at first since there's a lot of traffic near the restaurant, but we eventually get out of the worst of it. It takes about twenty-five minutes to get home in normal traffic, but not far from home the driver brakes suddenly until we come to a complete stop.

I straighten up and peer out the window. All the cars around us are stopped too.

"Traffic jam," I say to William, who hasn't straightened up but has lifted his head from where he was reclining it against the headrest. "Just wonderful."

There's a window between us and the driver's seat, obscured and soundproofed for privacy. I should use the intercom to talk, but I always feel weird doing it, so I roll down the dividing window instead.

Leaning forward, I ask Ray, "Do you know what's going on?"

Ray is a competent, beefy guy who used to be a Navy SEAL. He looks intimidating, but he's polite, good-natured, and easily amused. I've always liked him. "Sounds like there's a big accident about a mile ahead of us. Gonna be a while. Sorry."

"Not your fault. Hopefully they'll get it cleared quickly." I smile at him before I roll back up the window. Then I lean back against the seat, as close to William as I was before. "Well, that's just great. Glad I peed before I left the restaurant."

William's body shakes with a silent chuckle. "Yeah. That was smart."

"You don't need to go, do you?"

"Nah, I'm fine." He leans his head back and closes his eyes. There are shadows beneath them. He looks utterly exhausted.

I can't help it. I reach up to stroke his face gently. "Are you sure you're okay?"

"I'm fine," he says again, opening his eyes. His expression isn't annoyed or impatient. More curious than anything else. "Why do you keep asking?"

"I don't know. You just look..." I'm not sure how to put it in words. "I thought you would be... happier today."

"Yeah," he admits very softly. He's not meeting my eyes, but he wraps his arm around me again. "Me too."

I swallow over a lump and reach over to grab his free hand, stroking it with both of mine. "Do you not want all this responsibility anymore?"

"I still want it. It's exactly what I want." He clears his throat, pausing before he adds, "It feels like I'm finally starting to get everything I want."

"So what's the problem?"

"It doesn't change who I am. Even in a new situation, I'm still... me. And the truth is..."

When he trails off, I turn his head so he's looking down at me. "What's the truth, William?"

His voice is raw, thick, reluctant. "The truth is I'm scared shitless I'm going to lose everything I just barely have."

I know how he feels. Exactly how he feels. Because I feel the exact same way about him.

It feels like I've barely gotten my fingers wrapped around him, and he's going to be ripped out of my grip at any moment.

With a sympathetic noise in my throat, I pull him down enough to wrap my arms around him in a hug. It's awkward because of our seat belts. I end up taking mine off. After a minute, he pulls me into his lap so he can hold me more easily.

We sit that way for a long time. At one point, the car moves up a few feet but then comes to a dead stop again.

I don't want to move. I want to lean against William, his arms wrapped around me, his breath against my skin, for all of time. Safe. Protected. Cared for. Valued.

Forever.

When it feels like the mood of his hold starts to change, I turn my head so I can see his face. He's watching me—still tired but warmer than before.

Very warm.

"You're not thinking naughty thoughts, are you?" I ask, genuinely curious.

He laughs. "Why would you think that?"

"I don't know. You had a look in your eyes."

He pulls my face over so he can kiss me. Slow and thorough and leisurely. When he finally breaks away, he murmurs, "Well, who knows how long we're going to be stuck in this traffic jam?"

Giggling, I adjust my position. "Okay. I'm telling you right now, I'm not taking off my clothes in the back of this car. Tinted windows or no. But I'm happy to do something for you."

His lips part, and his eyes grow hot as I sink onto my knees on the floor of the back seat. The car is exceptionally roomy and always kept in pristine condition, so I'm not worried about my bare legs on the carpet. I do have to hike up my skirt.

"Don't do it only to satisfy me," William says, his eyes raking over me.

"I'm going to do it because I want to." I meet his eyes and wait for him to nod before I reach up to unfasten his belt.

There's a bit of unsexy maneuvering as I get his pants undone and pull them down enough to free his penis. He's already halfway aroused.

He groans softly as I stroke him. Closes his eyes for a minute but then opens them again. Focuses down on me as if he doesn't want to miss seeing anything.

I tease him with my fingers until he's fully erect. I'm familiar with his body now. He likes when I stroke my fingertips up the underside of his shaft and lightly massage his balls. There's a certain thrill to watching and feeling him grow under my touch. Harden and lengthen with ragged gasps and a slight shifting of his hips.

Beneath the thrill is a heavy clench below my belly. Not arousal but somehow akin. Ownership. A bone-deep recognition that he's mine—*mine*—to take care of this way.

When I glance up, he's watching me hotly, his eyes narrowed from heavy, languid lids. And he's still watching when I raise myself higher on my knees and lean forward so I can circle the head of him with my lips.

I give him a light suck that provokes a breathless exclamation from him.

He pulls a couple of pins out my chignon, letting it fall

loose over my shoulders before combing his fingers through the length. When I take more of him in my mouth, some of my hair falls forward, blocking my face, so he gathers it up in his fist and holds it in a loose ponytail so he can see what I'm doing to him.

I push his legs farther apart and maneuver my hand in place so I can rub his balls as I establish a steady rhythm with my mouth. Gradually the muscles of his thighs and stomach tense. The grip on my hair gets tighter. His breathing accelerates until it finally transforms into help-less, choppy moans.

I'm not sure I've ever in my life felt so powerful. So free. Like I'm flying and grounded and safe and free-falling all at the exact same time.

Taking as much of him as I can in my mouth, I suck hard a few times. Edge my fingers back so I can rub the sensitive spot behind his sac.

He lets out a loud, broken groan and jerks his hips a few times as he lets go. His shaft shudders in my mouth before he comes in several spurts.

I take him as best I can, coughing just slightly as I swallow a second time.

He lets go of my hair and moves his hand to cup my face. "You okay?" he rasps, fully relaxed now, soft and sated.

Letting him slip from my lips at last, I smile up at him. "Yeah. I'm good."

"Thank you, sweetheart."

"You're welcome."

He looks like he's about to go to sleep, so I'm genuinely surprised when he reaches down to pull me up from the floor and settle me on his lap again. I snuggle into him, breathing the familiar scent of him, exhilarated and terrified both that he smells exactly like home to me.

He nuzzles the crook of my neck, pressing a few clumsy kisses on my skin. "Can I take care of you now?"

I laugh softly. "You're exhausted, and I'm fine. Besides, I still don't much want to take off my clothes."

"I'm sure I can manage something with your clothes on. Aren't you turned on?"

I am definitely aroused. My cheeks are hotly red, and I'm perspiring lightly, and there's a deep clench of desire between my legs. But I told him the truth. I'm good right now. Physical desire is fairly far down on the list of emotions I'm feeling at the moment. "Kind of. But you really don't have to—"

I break off my unconvincing protestation when his hand slides between my legs. Before he touches me intimately, he asks, "Are you trying to be generous, or do you really not want me to get you off?"

He's genuinely asking. He doesn't want to go further until he's clear on what I want.

"I was trying to be generous," I admit. "I loved doing

that for you, so I don't need reciprocation. I wanted you to enjoy it. I'm honestly okay, but if you want to—"

I cut myself off again. This time with a sharp gasp when I feel his fingers slide beneath my underwear and stroke my hot arousal.

He flicks my clit. Adjusts my body to give him better access. Then parts me again with his fingers and slides one fully inside me.

I whimper and hide my face in his suit jacket. I know the barrier between the front and back of the car is sound-proofed, but I'm still a little self-conscious about Ray sitting only a few feet away.

"Do you think I don't enjoy doing this for you too?" William asks thickly. "Think about how you felt when you did this for me. That's how I feel with you."

I make a weird little sobbing sound, more from emotion than physical pleasure. Because it's so hard for me to believe it could be true.

He curls two fingers inside me and presses against my G-spot. My whole body jerks from the pleasure.

"I want to give you this, sweetheart. I want you to feel good. I want to watch you let go of everything you're always trying to hold together. I want to give you every-thing you need. I've never known anything like it before, how much I would want to take care of someone. How deeply the need is now rooted in my heart. I've never gotten to experience this before, so please don't take it away from me."

I'm sobbing for real now—with heightening pleasure and with helpless emotion and with a neediness I've never let myself feel before.

He tilts his head to kiss my hair, his hand pumping faster and harder. "You can trust me." He makes a weird sound, like he choked on a word. "Sweetheart, you can trust me enough to let go."

I'm sobbing into his jacket, smothering the sound as best I can. I'm not sure what's happening to me, why I'm falling apart all of a sudden like this. I wouldn't think I'd be capable of coming while wracked with emotion this way, but my body is still responding. A climax is growing slow and heavy, and my hips start moving instinctively, trying to ride his hand.

"That's right," he murmurs. "So good. You're so good. Just let go. You can let go for me. Let me give you this. Let me give you everything."

He pushes hard against my G-spot, and my spine arches dramatically as the pressure gets me over the edge.

I shake and sob through a powerful climax, coming apart completely on his lap. It lasts a long time, and he strokes and talks me through it, murmuring how good I'm doing, how much I need this, how all he wants is to give it to me.

When I've worked through the last of the spasms, I

collapse against him, limp and replete. He brushes kisses into my hair, rubs my back and one of my thighs until my breathing has finally evened out.

"Thank you," I mumble when I'm capable of speech. I lift my head when I realize the car is moving again. The traffic jam must be finally clearing.

"You're welcome." His voice is a little different now. Not as sexy but still tender. "I want you to trust me in everything. You need to know that."

I manage to nod. "Thank you," I say, wishing I could. Wishing life would allow it.

But he doesn't know what he's saying.

He wants Amber to trust him.

He doesn't love Jade. He doesn't even know her.

And he never will.

9

Two days later, William takes the entire Sunday off from work. We sleep in, go out to brunch, and then take a leisurely walk in a nearby park afterward.

The day is crisp, cool, and bright, and I enjoy the feel of the breeze and the sun on my face as William and I stroll, chatting occasionally and otherwise sharing a comfortable silence.

It feels real. Feels like home. Feels like I finally found someone I can share my life with. Someone I can take care of, who equally wants to take care of me.

If only there weren't a huge, overwhelming pile of garbage set right in the way of our future.

No matter how this feels right now, we won't get anywhere long-term unless we can somehow break through the mess.

Reality is rarely kind. I know that as well as anyone.

And the likelihood is that we'll get buried under the pile rather than managing to plow it away.

I brood for a few minutes, absorbed with the stray analogy.

"You okay?" William asks.

His light, familiar voice breaks me out of my reverie. "Yeah," I say with a smile. "Why do you ask?"

"Because I thought you were enjoying today, but you just now started feeling heavy."

It's unnerving how well he knows me. How easily he can read me. "Just random sober thoughts."

"Anything you'd like to share?" He slants me a quick look.

Of course I want to share it with him. But I feel that huge mess looming. It's too much. Too terrifying.

I've been feeling safe and happy for the first time in my life, and I'm not ready to give it up yet.

"Nah. Just random thoughts."

"Okay. But I'm happy to hear any thoughts you have even if they're random."

I'm relieved that his tone is still light, casual. He's not pushing, and his mood hasn't changed. I reach over and rub his back briefly. "Thanks. I'll keep that in mind."

"You want some ice cream?" he asks, nodding toward a cart on the corner of the park.

I perk up. "Yes!"

He takes my hand, easing me out of the way of a

jogging dad with a running stroller and then holding my hand as we make a beeline for the ice-cream cart.

We both get cones and find an empty bench to eat them. I giggle as I lick and nibble, trying to beat the melting of the ice cream. William eats his in bigger bites, but his eyes rarely leave my face.

If his expression wasn't so soft, I'd be self-conscious, but as it is, his look feels like a warm caress.

When we're done, he throws away our trash and then returns to the bench to wrap an arm around me. I lean against him, smiling as I close my eyes, relaxing against the familiar feel and scent of his body.

He's enjoying this too. I know he is. The man I met almost three months ago would never have spent a lazy Sunday like this.

I've been just as good for him as he's been for me.

"Sweetheart."

I can't tell if the word is a question or a random endearment. I adjust so I can peer up at his face.

He leans down to kiss me softly. Then holds my face. "Are you happy?"

My lips part. "Yes. I am. I have been." I swallow hard. "Have you?"

"Yes. Happier than I thought it was possible for me to be. But..."

When he trails off, my chest clenches. "But what?"

"But I'm feeling like there's a piece missing. I try to put

it aside like we agreed, but it's starting to nag at me. I'm wondering if you're ready to... unpress pause."

I can see it's hard for him to say that. To let himself be vulnerable enough to express his own feelings and needs.

So I treat his words very carefully even though my instinct is to push away in self-protection. I straighten up slowly, turning my head enough to press a light kiss against his palm. "I understand what you mean. I feel that way sometimes too. We can act like the... the mess we left behind isn't there, but it is."

"So is it all right if we move past this limbo?"

He's right. I know he's right. And it's what I want down deep too. But I know what it means. The huge, ugly truth is waiting for me to reveal, and it will tear everything we've started building down.

I can't get a word out of my throat as it tightens. My hands start to shake.

He must see my panic rising. "We don't have to do it all it once," he says quickly. "We can still take our time. I just don't want to be trapped in this artificial stasis. I want this to be... real."

His voice breaks slightly on the last word, and it goes right to my heart.

"I want that too." I reach up to cover his jaw with one of my hands. "I really do."

"Okay. I'm not pushing. I promise I'm not. But I'd like to be done with pause."

I nod, a lump in my throat strangling me. "Okay. We're done with pause."

He makes a guttural sound and pulls me into a tight hug. I return it, burying my face in his shirt.

He feels so human right now. So strong and breakable both. He's not only a blessing. He's also a deep responsibility.

I have to do right by him.

I must.

When I've pulled myself together, I force through the swell of rising panic. "I did want to... I needed to..."

The words get trapped in my throat, so I clear it. He loosens his arms and pulls back, lifting my face with an understated urgency. "You needed to what, sweetheart."

"To... say... to tell you—" This time I don't trail off. I break off abruptly when my eyes shift past his face.

And I see someone.

I see him. Mild demeanor. Slightly receding hairline. Wire-framed glasses. Expensive, casual clothes.

Montaigne.

I freeze as an icy wave slices through me. I move my eyes automatically back to William, but my vision has blurred and darkened. I can't see William's face. I can't see anything.

"What the fuck?" William mutters, his posture stiffening abruptly. "What happened? What's wrong? Tell me right now."

I can feel Montaigne across the park, leaning against a retaining wall. An arrogant smirk on his face.

He knows. He knows it's me and not Amber.

He knows he's found me at last.

I'm shaking now—so much my teeth chatter. "Take me... Please take me home." It takes every ounce of control I possess to get the words out.

William gets up immediately, reaching down to pull me to my feet. He glances around at our surroundings, and I can tell he's about to make a more thorough search for whatever triggered my reaction.

He can't look. From a distance, maybe Montaigne won't have seen my visceral reaction to him. I only glanced at him for a few seconds. But if William stares around defensively, then Montaigne will know for sure I recognize him.

Amber isn't supposed to know him.

With a whimper of fear, I say, "No. Don't. Just please take me home."

His expression twists, like it takes an internal battle, but he puts an arm around me and guides me out of the park and onto the city sidewalk.

I have no idea if Montaigne follows or not. I don't dare to look.

To my relief, William doesn't try interrogating me on the walk back. We make it to our building. Then to the private elevator. When the doors shut, I close my eyes and lean back against the wall with a helpless whimper.

I'd thought it was over. I'd hoped I was safe.

But it will never be over.

I'm back where I was a few months ago, trapped behind walls, unable to walk freely in the world for fear of being watched.

For fear of soon being harmed or killed.

Everything changed for me, but then nothing changed at all.

"Sweetheart, please." William's voice rasps. He puts an arm around me and pulls me against him as the elevator ascends floors. "Tell me what's going on. I'm seriously about to lose it."

I can't make my voice work. I can't stop shaking. I hide my face in his shirt for the minute it takes us to reach our floor.

I barely register stepping off the elevator into our entryway. I'm pretty sure I slide off my shoes automatically and let my purse slide onto the floor beside me.

With a hand on my back, William guides me into the media room and helps me sit on the couch. I fold my body up so I'm hugging my legs and let my teeth chatter again.

William sits beside me and waits for a minute until my shivering has lessened. Then I'm finally able to focus on his face.

He's sweating visibly. His jaw and shoulders are tense. His brown eyes are wildly urgent.

I have to tell him soon—now—or I'm half-convinced he'll literally explode.

"I..." I take a ragged breath that hurts my throat and push through. "I used to have a stalker."

He blinks. "A stalker. When?"

I open my mouth and realize my dilemma. If I tell him the accurate timeline, then all my lies will come out. "A... a while back. He wouldn't stop. I tried reporting him, but he has friends in the department and labeled me a nut. I tried moving. Twice. He always found me. I thought—coming here, I thought I'd finally shaken him. But... but..."

William sucks in a long, sharp breath through his teeth. "He was in the park? Just now?"

I nod, trembling again and then finally starting to cry.

"What does he look like?"

It's not the question I expect, and it's easier to answer than the more predictable queries. "He's about five eleven. In his thirties. Wire glasses with a receding hairline."

"What was he wearing today? Did you notice?"

I nod, blinking away tears. "Khakis and a blue shirt unbuttoned over a T-shirt."

"Is it all right if I step out for just a minute? It won't be long."

I have no idea what's happening here, but I nod anyway. He can do anything he wants. Just his being here when I need him is more than I ever prayed for before.

He strokes my face. Then closes his fingers around a

bunch of my hair and slides it down the length of it as he stands up. "I'll be close."

I sit huddled up on the couch as he walks out of the media room and into the hallway. I don't know how far he goes, but it can't be far because I can hear the low murmur of his voice and occasionally catch words.

He's on the phone. Giving instructions to someone. Telling them to search the park and around our building for someone matching the description I gave him. Then he gives more instructions—about ramping up our security. Getting a regular rotation of bodyguards.

For me.

I start crying again before he ends his conversation.

It's not long before he comes back and lowers himself to the couch beside me. He leans against the back and pulls me to him, wrapping both arms around me.

I sprawl against his chest, halfway on his lap, and I cry some more. He holds me tight, murmuring out rough assurances. About how it's going to be all right. He's got me. He's going to keep me safe. I can trust him. He won't let me down.

Everything I need to hear. Everything I've been desperate to hear for so long.

And never have. Not once in my life.

When I've cried myself out, I stay reclining limply against him. He's loosened his arms now and is gently stroking my hair and my back.

Finally he murmurs thickly, "Is this why you... you came to me?"

"Yes. I needed... I just needed to feel safe. I'm so sorry. I... I used you. I'm so, so sorry."

"Don't be. I understand. I'm glad to know. I never understood..." He makes a weird sound in his throat. "I never understood it, but this makes everything clear."

He sounds so relieved. Almost overcome. Like it's the answer he's been waiting for forever. And it breaks my heart because he's wrong.

Everything still isn't clear to him.

He doesn't know all there is to know.

I have to tell him. I was about to back in the park. I'm sure I would have actually gotten it said this time had Montaigne not shown up right at the worst moment.

Fate. It feels like fate.

I try to collect my former momentum and drive to tell the truth, but I can barely lift my head, much less give my final confession.

The one that will take everything that matters away from me.

But it's wrong. It's selfish. It's thinking of myself rather than William.

And I love him. More than I've ever loved myself.

I might not be able to say everything right now, but I can say something. The first step to the truth coming out.

So I make myself say it.

"You can..." I choke. Literally choke. I have to sit up and cough until tears stream out of my eyes.

He pats my back and waits until I'm able to speak again.

"You can tell your security guys the stalker's name is..."

I don't pause on purpose, but I almost get choked again. William has stiffened, leaning forward, like he's poised on the edge of a cliff.

"Vince Montaigne."

Maybe it doesn't seem like much of a confession, but I know what will happen afterward. He'll give the name to his security. They'll investigate. Get background information and photographs. They'll learn he's from Houston and has lived there all his life.

Amber has never lived in Houston.

It won't make sense. But William will remember Detective Curtis, the police detective from Houston who was looking for Amber's twin sister, Jade.

It won't take him long to put the pieces together.

The truth might as well be out right now.

I feel sick and exhausted and battered and torn.

And a little bit relieved.

The end is finally in sight.

The security guys find no sign or trace of Montaigne.

Not for a moment do I believe I imagined his presence. He was there for sure. He left after we did, but he'll be back. Now that he knows where I am and what I'm doing, he'll try to start back up his stalking campaign.

Or do worse.

William asks for my permission to assign me a bodyguard for close protection. I don't care if it means someone will be at my heels for the foreseeable future. I agree without the slightest hesitation. I'd rather be safe and a little bit stifled than to be dead or kidnapped.

And I actually have hope now that Montaigne will be caught. Stopped. He's no longer up against a defenseless woman without connections. He's up against William Worthing and his high-paid security team.

Surely something will finally happen.

I'm exhausted after my panic and the emotional effort it's taken to admit this much of the truth to William, so I end up falling asleep on the couch.

I wake up with my head in William's lap. He's working on his phone and stroking my hair gently. It feels so good. So intimate.

Like I'm being taken care of.

"Hey," I mumble, shifting my position so I can see up at his face.

"Hey." He smiles down at me, looking rather tired himself.

"You should have taken a nap too."

"Too wired for that."

"Are you?" I find the energy to sit up, folding my legs beneath me. "Are you okay? Are you upset by all this?"

"Not upset."

I pause, waiting for him to clarify.

He gives a dry, breathy laugh. "I'm having to fight down all these intense protective instincts that I never knew I possessed but have all somehow leaped into urgency. Like I'm ready to fight the world off to keep you safe."

I choke on a little sob and lean over to give him a hug. I have no idea what I can say to that—anything that will meet how much the words meant to me—so I squeeze him instead.

He tightens his arms around me too. Mumbles, "I keep telling myself I've done everything I can do so I need to calm the hell down. But I can't. I won't. It's frankly kind of embarrassing. I swear I could get into a damned fistfight right now."

I giggle into his shoulder and then pull back enough to kiss him softly. "Thank you."

"For what? For feeling like a fucking caveman for no rational reason?"

"There is reason. And you'll never know how much it means that you want to protect me. I've... I've never had anyone do that for me before."

He shakes his head and cups my face. "Well, you do now."

I still don't have words to shape what I'm feeling right now. So instead, I kiss him again. This time he grabs the back of my head and holds on, deepening the kiss until my head spins.

Clutching at his shoulders, I get pushed backward with the intensity of the kiss until I'm lying on the couch with him on top of me. My legs are bent, folded up on each side of his hips, and his tongue is deep in my mouth, thrusting with a rhythm that matches the primal rocking of his hips.

It takes only a couple of minutes for him to get hard. I feel the bulge growing against my middle. His arousal fuels my own. I started the kiss overwhelmed with emotion, but gradually my physical need intensifies to match the emotional. My hands fumble with his shirt and his hair, trying desperately to pull him closer and to pull off his clothes at the same time.

I want to feel his skin. I want to feel him all over. I want to feel him inside me.

It feels like I'm drowning in how much I *want*.

He's equally needy, almost clumsy as he devours my mouth and feels my body wherever he can reach. The kiss lasts a long time. Then he moves down my body, pushing up my top and pulling my breasts out of my bra cups so he can tease and suck the nipples.

The pressure between my thighs deepens. Heightens. I gasp and writhe under his ministrations, eventually edging up my hips so I can pull off the pale gray pants I'm wearing. They're Amber's. Expensive with a thick, stretchy material and a skinny fit. I have some trouble peeling them off over my butt and thighs and accidentally clobber William's belly in the process.

He grunts and lifts his head. "Ow."

Since it's clear I didn't really hurt him, I collapse into giggles. "I'm sorry! I was having trouble getting these stupid pants off."

"Well, why didn't you just ask." He's hiding a smile as he grabs the waistband and pulls them down my legs with obnoxious ease, taking my underwear with them.

I make a face at him. "You had a more advantageous position than I did."

He drops the pants off the side of the couch with a low chuckle. "Did I?"

"Yes. You did." I'm tempted to stick my tongue out at him, but I manage to resist the impulse. "I can usually take my pants off just fine."

Laughter is still vibrating through his body as he leans down to kiss me again. "That's good to know."

I have a fleeting flash of worry about the lovely, pristine sofa, so I grab a throw blanket and slide it beneath my bottom so whatever we do doesn't mess up the upholstery.

That makes him laugh even more.

I'm torn between my fit of giggles and pleasure at the kiss. For some reason, the fond amusement makes all my other feelings more intense. The emotions and the physical sensations. It's not long before I'm completely absorbed in the embrace again, and I get more excited as he starts moving down my body again.

He's still smiling as he nuzzles between my thighs, opening my folds with his fingers and then teasing my clit with his tongue. I buck up off the couch at the surge of pleasure. Then grab for his head as he starts working me over with his mouth.

The pleasure grows for a couple of minutes until I'm whimpering helplessly. Then he sucks hard on my clit, and I come apart completely.

When my shaking, moaning, and gasping finally fade, he lifts his head and smiles down at me again. I don't resent the smugness even a little.

I pull him down into a hug. "Thank you for that."

"You're welcome." He's already unfastening his trousers and pushing down his boxers enough to free his erection. "You ready for more?"

"Yes, I'm ready." I feel an odd kind of pleasure as I help him position himself between my legs. I love that he needs me so much. That I can do this not just for me but for him. I love that I can meet his needs. So it's more than affection and arousal—it's a primitive kind of satisfaction that's filling me as he uses his hand to line himself up and then slides himself home inside me.

He groans low and long, closing his eyes and tightening his lips.

I slide my hands up to hold on to his face, my breathing accelerating from the tight, delicious penetration.

After a minute, he opens his eyes and smiles down at me. "You'd think eventually I'd get used to how it feels to be inside you, but I haven't yet."

I flush all the way down to my chest, momentarily afraid I might melt away from warm sentiment.

He leans down to kiss me gently. "It feels like I've been waiting for you my whole life."

"Me too," I admit. "Me too."

He's always been a reserved man, but something has changed in him. Slowly he's been opening up to me, but now there appears to be no barriers left. He's giving me all of him, all of who he is. Not just in his words but in the way he's gazing down at me.

Like everything in his heart—all his warmth and depth and faith and commitment and strength and vulnerability —all of it is there in his eyes.

It's so much. Almost too much. My face twists as I try to handle the surge of emotion.

"You okay?" he asks thickly, his expression changing. "You still want this?"

"Yes! Please, I still want it. Don't stop. Don't ever stop."

He makes a choked sound and begins to thrust, building a fast, needy rhythm that matches everything else I'm sensing in him.

It feels so good. So needed. I pump my hips to match his rhythm and clutch handfuls of the shirt he's still wearing. We move together, breathing fast and loud until our pants turn into little grunts. Mine get more stretched as pleasure builds at my center, and his get louder and more animalistic.

He's letting himself go. Completely. No holding back. His motion gets harder, and it's exactly what I want to feel.

"Please," I hear myself rasping. "Please, William!"

"What do you need, sweetheart?" He has to force the words out because he's pretty far gone.

"I need... I need... I need you to love me."

I had no plans to say those words. No idea how they came out. No clue how to feel now that they've been said.

He makes another throaty sound and tosses his head.

I dig my fingernails into the back of his neck as an orgasm finally crests. I cry out as I fall into release.

He's not far behind me, jerking his hips a few last times before he lets out a loud sound that's almost a bellow.

I've never heard him like that before. I never knew he could let go so much.

I never knew I could either.

When his motion finally slows to a few uneven rocks of his hips, he buries his face against the crook of my neck. Mumbles a barely audible, "I do."

We lie tangled together for a long time afterward. At first I can process nothing except the lingering pleasure and the depth of what I feel for William, but eventually other realities begin to sneak in.

He's very heavy. Moisture is leaking out from where we are joined, and it's not exactly comfortable. I'm glad I used the throw blanket.

I heard what he said.

When I shift slightly, he lifts his head and pushes himself up by straightening his arms. He's peering down at me, like he's waiting for something.

"What...?" My voice breaks, so I try again. "What do you want?"

He takes a long breath and lets it out. "I want you to trust me. All the way."

I'm surprised by this admission. I stare up at him, trying to process it, figure out what it means.

"I... I do," I say at last, realizing it's true. It has to be true. There's no other way to understand the state of my heart and mind.

His face breaks slightly. "Then do it, sweetheart. Trust me. All the way." He kisses me softly and then heaves himself up off the couch and walks with a slight limp toward the bathroom. I hear the door shut.

I sit up too, pulling on my top and panties and thinking everything through.

He loves me. There's no way for me to disbelieve that.

And I trust him now. I have to. It's become a bone-deep truth of my life.

Which means there's one more thing left for me to do.

I get up and walk to the hallway, waiting outside the bathroom door. After a minute, I hear the toilet flush and then the water running in the sink.

The door opens, and he's come to a stop in the doorway, his face slightly damp from where he must have splashed water on it and his expression obviously surprised.

"I have to tell you something," I blurt out before I can rethink or change my mind.

He freezes. *Freezes*. Finally whispers, "What is it?"

I expect the words to get caught in my throat, but this time they don't. They come out clearly. My heart hammers so much I can barely hear myself say, "I'm not Amber. I'm Jade."

10

———

I'M NOT SURE HOW I EXPECT WILLIAM TO REACT. I'VE imagined this moment hundreds of times and have never settled on a response that felt true and inevitable. Anger, shock, outrage, betrayal, deep hurt. One of those or a combination of all of them. It's part of why it's been such a terrifying step for me to take.

I have absolutely no idea what will happen now.

He doesn't do anything I might have expected him to do. He stays very still, staring at me fixedly until his knees buckle just slightly. He sways almost imperceptibly and takes a quick step to steady himself.

I run over instinctively, wrapping a supportive arm around him. He looks slightly sheepish and too pale as we make our way back to the couch and sit down.

He takes a couple of deep breaths until his normal

color returns. Then, to my astonishment, his lips twitch up slightly. "Thank you for finally telling me."

It takes several seconds for my mind to catch up. To make sense of his expression, of what it must mean.

Then I gasp dramatically. "You already knew?"

His eyes are soft, warmly amused. Nothing sharp or bitter. "Yes, I already knew."

I'm hit with a tidal wave of shock and relief and confusion. "Then why... why didn't you... How is this...?" I can't complete a sentence. Or a thought. I'm shaking and have to twist my hands together to keep them still. "Why...?"

He reaches over and covers my trembling hands with one of his. He doesn't say anything, but the touch is soothing, calming, gives me strength.

"You've known the whole time?"

"No," he admits, dropping his eyes almost ruefully. "Not the whole time. Not anywhere close to the whole time. When that detective stopped by to question you, I finally figured it out. I'd known something wasn't right—that something had changed—but none of my hundreds of possible theories were panning out. Discovering Amber had an identical twin sister was the last piece of the puzzle I needed. Finally the whole situation started making sense."

"Why didn't you tell me?" I ask, still feeling disoriented and on the verge of tears.

William looks at me quietly with those brown eyes that

have always been as speaking as anything he says with words.

I'm finally processing the significance of what he's told me. All this time, as I've been desperately trying to play the role of Amber—as I've been wracked by guilt about having to deceive and betray him—he's known all along. He's been playing along, letting me stumble through the steps of a losing game.

"I can't believe it," I rasp, leaning forward and staring at the floor. "I've been so upset about the whole thing—so torn up about lying to you—and you were just... just..."

My tone isn't angry or accusatory. I don't feel anger at all. I have no idea what I feel.

"I wasn't enjoying it either," he says quietly. "Not the deception. But I didn't know what was happening, and I needed to figure you out."

I blink. Slant a look at him. "Oh. Yes. That makes sense."

"You were a stranger, living with me, pretending to be my fiancée. I knew you were a better person than Amber. I knew that without doubt. But I still didn't know what your motive was. Why you were doing it. I couldn't... I couldn't let down my guard until I did."

I lower my eyes again. "Of course you couldn't. There's no way you should have trusted me. I would have done the same thing. I'm really sorry about the whole thing. I was desperate and didn't know what else to do. But I didn't want to lie to you. I never wanted to lie."

"I concluded that. I had my people investigating you, but I couldn't get to the real story. I knew you must have been desperate. In danger somehow. But the only stories I was uncovering were that you were mentally unbalanced and paranoid and lashing out against innocent men."

I choke on a familiar outrage. "Those were Montaigne's lies."

"Yes. I know that now. But I didn't know about Montaigne back then. Even then, I had trouble believing it. That I could have so completely fallen for..." He shakes his head. "I knew I hadn't heard the real story yet, but I needed the real story. So yes, I played along. I didn't tell you what I knew. And I kept waiting for you to finally tell me the truth."

I'm shaking again—with a different emotion this time. "I'm so sorry, William. I wouldn't blame you if you never forgave me."

"I've already forgiven you. I won't say it didn't hurt, and I won't say I was never angry, but the more I got to know you, the more I understood. And when you told me about Montaigne, I understood everything. I probably would have done the same thing if I was in your situation. I assume the swap was Amber's idea?"

"Yes. I never would have dreamed of such a ludicrous scheme. She wanted..."

"Money." He says the words simply, no particular resonance.

"Yes. I assume that was her main motivation. I thought —" I shake my head with a bitter little laugh. "I thought she was actually trying to help me. That maybe we could finally reconcile. Even after all this time, all the ways she's proved she doesn't care about me anymore, I still believed... But yes, I think she wanted escape while still getting the money she thinks she deserves. I assume in another month, she'll reappear and want to swap back so she can marry you and then end it and get the settlement laid out in the contract."

"Yes. That would be my guess too." He sighs and leans back against the couch, wrapping an arm around me and bringing me with him. "We did discover that she'd managed to access one of my accounts and must be using that money for her spending in the meantime."

"What? Seriously? And she thought she could get away with it?"

"She was smart. If I hadn't learned the truth about her and gone looking for suspicious activity, I might not have found it until too late. She's sharp."

"I assume there's a man involved." I'm not even hurt that it's my sister we're talking about. I'm far too exhausted and burned out to feel wounded at the moment.

"Oh yes. It's someone from her gym."

"Seriously?"

"Yes. That much was easy to uncover."

"And she doesn't know that we know?"

"I don't think so."

"Well then."

His chest rises and falls with a sardonic huff. "Yeah."

We sit together in silence for a few minutes. I nestle against him, astonished and deeply relieved I'm still allowed to take comfort from him this way.

After a minute of searching my memory, I say, "You haven't called me Amber recently."

"Not since I found out you're Jade. Honestly, I almost slipped up a time or two."

"I had no idea. I thought you just wanted to call me..."
Sweetheart.

That's what he's been calling me for weeks now.

"So when you suggested we put all our mess on pause, you knew exactly what that meant to me. You knew it meant my real identity?"

"Yes. That was for me as much as for you. I knew you were torn up about it. I could see it so clearly. You tried to run away after we first had sex, and I understood why. It was important to me that you tell me the truth—that you get to the point where you could take that step—but I also needed to know that there was something worth... worth fighting for. So the pause helped me as much as you. I could be with you without constantly obsessing about what it all meant. But it wasn't enough. Gradually all the questions kept coming back to me until I was dying to get the truth out one way or another."

"Yes. That's how I was feeling too. It worked for a while —and it gave me a safety net—but it was always temporary. Artificial. But I couldn't get over the absolute certainty that telling you the truth would mean I'd lose you."

"I don't know why you thought that. What did I do to make you doubt me?"

"You didn't do anything." I lift my head to meet his eyes. "It wasn't your fault. It was me. I've lived..." I swallow over the break in my voice. "I've lived all my life with the people I've loved and trusted the most betraying me. My dad. And Amber. Even a few months ago, I fell for the hope that Amber might... might return my love and trust. Only to be crushed again. The people I love don't love me back. They can't be trusted. That's what life has taught me. But I was wrong to apply that lesson to you. I'm sorry."

He wraps both arms around me in a hug, holding me tightly as I shake against him. He doesn't say anything, but it feels like he understands.

And it means everything.

We hug for a long time, and then we both relax back against the sofa. His arm is still around me. "So what now?" I ask softly.

"I... don't know. What do you want?"

"Should we...?" I want to blurt out I'm desperately in love with him and never want to be apart for the rest of our lives. But my deception has just come to light. He's forgiven me evidently, but he must still be conflicted. He cares about me, but I can't simply assume that he wants exactly what I want. So giving us both a little time and space to figure things out seems the safest route. "Should we take a little time to process everything? And then decide what we want?"

"Yes," he answers immediately, no hesitation or reluctance. "That sounds like a good plan. No pressure. No demands."

"Okay. Good." I turn my head and press a little kiss against his shirt. "Thank you."

"You'll stay here, right?" he asks after a few seconds, the first trace of uncertainty in his tone. "I know you mentioned space, but you don't want to go somewhere else do you?"

"No. Not really. I mean, as long as it's okay with you."

"I'd like you to stay. If only because it will be safer for you. Montaigne is still out there, and we need to deal with him before you'll really be safe. After that, if you decide you want to go, then of course..."

"Yeah. I agree."

I can't imagine myself wanting to go. To leave. Not William and not this apartment.

It's the closest thing to home I've ever had.

~

The next day, I open the oven to check on how my lasagna is coming along.

I've spent an hour working on it, going through the detailed steps of an elaborate recipe mostly to distract myself from everything else on my mind. The lasagna still needs to cook for another half hour, but it's already looking and smelling delicious. Part of me is quite pleased with my evident culinary success.

The rest of me is still confused and anxious about all the recent developments.

We spent most of the day talking to lawyers and Houston-based FBI agents and Internal Affairs in the Houston police. I'm not sure what exactly will happen with Montaigne, but we've got a restraining order against him at least. And Detective Curtis is being put under the microscope, which is nothing more than he deserves.

William is working in his home office now. He got behind because all of this ate up so much of the day. He's been quiet and composed and gentle, but I can't help but wonder how he's feeling.

He was so sweet and genuine yesterday, but today he's been mostly professional. Maybe he's pulling back. Rethinking.

He's allowed, although the idea makes me want to fall apart.

I'm not really sure how I should act with him now that things have changed. Normally, I'd ask if he wants to have dinner with me. But maybe he wants more space. Maybe he doesn't feel like eating dinner with me.

I give a shrug and head to his office anyway. It would be rude not to ask, and he has to have dinner sometime after all.

I knock on his closed door and open it at his greeting.

"Hey," I say with what I hope is a casual smile. "I made lasagna. If you're hungry, you could join me. Or eat it in here. Or whatever."

The invitation doesn't sound as breezy as I hoped, but William smiles at me anyway. "Sure. Sounds good."

When I see him start to close out a document on his computer, I add, "It won't be ready for a half hour or so, so you can finish up what you're working on. I just wanted to know if I should make a salad or not."

"I was done anyway." He gets up and walks toward where I'm standing in the doorway. He's wearing gray trousers and a black long-sleeved shirt. "I'll help with the salad."

I can't suppress a surprised smile as he walks with me back to the kitchen.

We work on washing lettuce and cutting vegetables together with companionable ease. We chat about inconsequential things—not about how we've spent the past several weeks lying to each other. And I'm feeling pleased —almost giddy—when the lasagna is ready and we set the table out on the terrace to eat.

The lasagna is a definite success, and I enjoy it even more since I spent so long making it. The terrace is lit with a subtle, well-designed lighting scheme and the candles on the table, and William's expression looks unusually warm in the soft light.

He smiles at me like he doesn't hate me. Like he doesn't resent me. Like he really understands why I lied to him.

And I can't blame him for not trusting me immediately and therefore not telling me when he discovered my real identity.

Ridiculously, it feels like we could have been any other couple having dinner together early in a relationship, like we're really starting to get to know each other. And I have the same kind of excited quivers in my chest and belly as I would have on a date that was going really well.

I try to remind myself that, despite the feelings that have developed between us, there still might be no future here. He's a supremely guarded man, and he might put back up his walls at any moment. But I can't seem to take my wise mental reminders to heart. It feels like we're on a date, like there might be hope.

We've finished the bread, lasagna, and salad and are finishing off the last of the red wine when we fall into a comfortable silence. William has been gazing out on the lit cityscape, obviously wrapped up in his own reflections. I'm watching him, thinking how incredibly attractive he is and how I've never met anyone who was as deep and complex and sensitive and generous as he is—no matter how much he might try to hide those characteristics.

William looks back over at me without warning, catching me in a besotted gaze. My cheeks flush slightly, but I manage a wry smile.

One corner of his mouth lifts in an answering expression, and it's one of those moments of intense connection that are indescribable but unmistakable. Like we are sharing something real, deep, in the locking of our eyes.

"You don't have to look so worried, Jade. I'm not angry with you. I was for a while, but I could tell the lying was difficult for you—that it went against your nature, that you didn't want to trick me that way. Once I got a sense of who you were, I could read you and I knew you weren't doing it to hurt me."

"I wasn't," I say hurriedly. "I promise I didn't want to hurt you. The more I got to know and... and like you, the more I hated myself for having to play the role. I hope you can forgive me."

He meets my eyes again. "I told you. I already have."

Something in my chest relaxes, and I feel another irrational surge of hope.

But my sense of irony overcomes the flood of sentiment, and I say with a quirk of my mouth, "Well, to tell you the truth, I'm still a little angry at you—for making me suffer for so long after you found out who I was."

William laughs softly, low in his throat. "You're just

annoyed that I came out on top in our little game—that I outplayed you."

I shoot him a glare of mock indignation. "Don't go down that road, or I'll bring up how long I *was* able to play you." It's a deep relief that he was able to tease about the issue since it convinces me he's telling the truth about not holding it against me.

I think about the first few weeks before Detective Curtis showed up and William realized who I really am. Then I think about how he's acted since.

"Were you—?" I cut off the spontaneous question before I even get it spoken, my cheeks warming with a deep flush.

William's brows draw together at the shift in mood. "Was I what?"

"It's nothing."

"What do you want to know, Jade?" He leans forward slightly, his skin flickering warmly with the light from the candle.

I give a half shrug. "Were you... were you into Amber? Is that why you agreed to the arrangement with her?"

His shoulders stiffen slightly, clearly surprised by the unexpectedly intimate question.

"You don't have to tell me," I add in a rush, filling the awkward silence. "I know it's private. It's no big deal. I was just wondering. About... about..."

"I thought she was beautiful. One of the most beautiful women I've ever met. That much is real."

I blush since I look exactly like her.

"But no, I wasn't into her. In fact, the more I got to know her, the less attractive I found her. I'm not sure if I can even explain it." He gives me a slightly sheepish look.

"I think it makes sense. Who people are always affects our attraction to them—one way or another."

"That's why I was so bewildered when suddenly I was attracted to her again." He huffs softly. "I couldn't make any sense of it. Why do I suddenly want to tear this woman's clothes off when I don't even really like her?"

I stifle a giggle, both nervous and amused by his bone-dry tone. "You were attracted to her again?"

"To you. But I believed it was her. It really threw me for a loop. Then you were acting different—so completely unlike her. At first I bought that she was genuinely trying to turn over a new leaf, but I never felt settled about it. Something was definitely wrong."

"So when did you start to suspect?"

"I didn't know enough to suspect anything specific. Just a general sense that something wasn't right. I was a mess. Consumed by lust that came out of nowhere—plus slowly falling for a woman I was sure I didn't like. Loving all the time we spent together but constantly questioning why it was happening." He gives me a quirk of a smile, rubbing his jaw. "I was a complete disaster. Then that detective showed up and announced Amber had a twin sister. Everything clicked into place. Of course that was what happened. It explained everything. The woman I'd been falling for wasn't Amber at all. After that, I was also a disaster. Just for another reason."

I can't help but laugh again, melting with pleasure over his self-deprecating admission. "You hid it well. I knew you were confused, but you always seemed to have yourself together. I've never met anyone so completely in control of himself."

He shakes his head. "It was all an act."

"And all that time you knew who I was and didn't say anything. I'm still not sure I'm okay with that." My tone is light, playful. He surely knows I'm teasing.

"You'll have to let me know what I can do to make up for it."

"Oh yeah?"

He slants me a hot look. "And then I'll let you know what you can do for lying to me for months."

I choke on a laugh and reach over to squeeze his hand. "You can let me know anytime. I'm happy to oblige."

I'm suddenly worried I've said too much. Been too forward. But I'm also excited about being that way. I feel silly and self-conscious and pleased and nervous at the same time. "Anyway."

"Anyway."

We fall into silence again.

"What about you?" William asks after a long pause.

I'm not exactly sure what he's asking, but I answer it anyway. "I was a complete disaster too. From the very beginning. At first I was mostly terrified. But then you weren't at all what I thought you would be. I started to like you. Then more than like you. Then I had to come to terms with the fact that I'd fallen for the man I was deceiving—and there was no way he'd ever forgive me."

"Well, he has. Forgiven you."

I nod and swallow hard, dropping my eyes. "Thank you."

Feeling like I might have revealed too much, I clear my throat and stand up, beginning to gather up the dishes. He helps me carry the dishes back into the kitchen. Although we can leave things for Greta, it feels lazy and sloppy to me, and neither of us like mess hanging around until the next day. We rinse them off and put them in the dishwasher.

When we put the last dish away, I turn to look at William, feeling self-conscious again. He appears unusually relaxed and domestic—and absolutely scrumptious with his black shirt slightly damp in spots from rinsing the dishes.

I part my lips to say something but then have no idea what to say.

He's gazing down at me, his eyes hot and deep. "What is it?"

My body tightens at the texture in his voice and at the sudden realization that we can have sex if we want. My cheeks burn and my blood starts to race with excitement and desire. "Nothing," I say, my voice cracking on the one word.

"What is it?" he asks again, his head inclining toward me, like he's trying to see into my soul.

My breath is coming out in uneven pants now, and a deep ache has tightened between my legs.

His questioning expression transforms into something else. He bends toward me all the way, his lips closing on mine.

The thrilled tension explodes inside me. I wrap my arms around his neck instinctively and open my mouth to the advance of his tongue. I moan as the kiss deepens and moan again when he makes a guttural sound in response.

He pushes me back against the counter, pressing the lean length of his body against mine. He's hard and hot and eager, and I rub myself shamelessly against him, arousal overwhelming me so quickly it aches.

I arch against the counter as William's lips move hungrily against mine, and I'm gasping desperately when he finally tears his mouth away.

"Oh God!" I try to make my mind work enough to figure out what's happening. Vaguely I realize that the kiss probably shouldn't have happened. We aren't together for real, no matter how much I might want it to be. "I'm sorry."

"Are you?" William asks, his face still only inches from mine and his hot eyes gazing down at me. "I'm not."

I'm not sure how it happens, but we end up back in the bedroom.

After the initial kiss in the kitchen, a swell of lust overwhelms us both. Shuddering with the knowledge that William wants me, wants to be with *me*, I give myself up to the feeling.

We tear off our clothes and tumble into bed, kissing and caressing with frantic need.

When he slides himself inside me, I arch up and gasp out his name.

"Jade," William mumbles against my skin, his face buried in my neck as he holds himself so tensely he's shaking with it. "Jade. Jade."

I arch again in pleasure at the sound of his saying my name.

He's filling me completely—tight and aching and unbearably good. And I'm flushed with heat and urgency and already clawing at his shoulders.

When he begins to thrust at last, we build up a fast, hungry rhythm—William grunting out primitive sounds of effort and pleasure and me biting my lower lip to keep from crying out too loudly.

I can't restrain the impulse for long, but it doesn't seem to matter. William is just as out of control as I am. We move eagerly together, our damp skin clinging and our bodies slapping on each instroke.

Every time he pushes into me, William rasps out my name, and every time I hear it, I cry out, "Yes!"

I'm on the verging of coming when I meet and hold his gaze. His eyes are hot and needy, and they don't look away from me.

He's seeing *me*. He's making love to *me*. I come on the knowledge.

He follows quickly, my clenching and shuddering pulling him into climax as well.

I cling to him as I come down, my chest aching with breathlessness and my body so hot I think I might melt. But I love the feel of him—his heated, sated weight on top of me, the way he seems to have let himself go completely.

In a way he almost never does.

William buries his face in the crook of my neck again and mumbles against my throat, "Jade. Jade."

I lift my neck into his fumbling kisses. "Oh God, William, that was so good."

He murmurs his agreement, still pressing his lips against my flushed skin.

"I'm not sure how we ended up here," I admit at last, trying to wrap my mind around exactly how it happened.

We were eating lasagna, then cleaning up, then ended up in bed together.

William raises his head, groaning softly as if it was too heavy to lift. "Aren't you? I know exactly how we ended up here."

I can't help but smile. "You do?"

"Do you really not know I love you, Jade?"

I writhe in pleasure at the words. "Really?"

He rolls his eyes as I beam up at him.

"Well, I didn't want to assume that what we said and did when we were lying to each other would stay exactly the same."

"It's not exactly the same. It's better. It's... truer."

I gulp and nod up at him tearfully. "Good. Because I love you too."

He leans down to kiss me softly. "I was hoping you would say that."

I pull him down into a hug, my legs still bent up around his hips. There's more I want to say, more I want to ask him, but it isn't necessary immediately.

For the moment, things feel exactly right.

I wake up the next morning hot and a little bit sore. My arm is asleep and is tingling painfully, and I'm trapped in an awkward position.

It takes me a moment to process where I am and why I'm so uncomfortable. I'm in bed with William. Although we cleaned up after we had sex last night, we fell asleep together later. And I'm now pressed up against him—which explains why I'm so hot. He's lying on one of my arms, and he's holding me tightly, preventing me from moving.

I moan uncomfortably and wriggle, trying to dislodge myself from his body.

William grunts and tenses against me, signaling that he's waking up too. His arms loosen.

"Help," I say, pulling at the arm that's still trapped beneath him.

He rolls over, and I sigh in relief at my freedom, shaking my arm to restore circulation.

"You all right?" His voice is still thick with sleep.

A quick glance at the clock shows it's just after five in the morning. The room is dim. "Yeah. My arm's just asleep."

He nods and stretches, looking relaxed and almost debauched with his softened features, bare chest, and sprawled position on the wrinkled sheets. "Everything else all right?" he asks after a moment, his eyes scrutinizing my face carefully.

I frown at him, immediately understanding what he's asking. "Do you think I would change my mind overnight? That I would regret what we did?" I'm quite sure my expression indicates my outrage at his ludicrous question.

His lips twitch slightly. "Just checking."

Since I feel kind of icky, I get up to go to the bathroom, wash my hands and face, and get some coffee for both me and William.

William is a perpetually early riser, but he doesn't seem to be in a hurry today. We drink our coffee in contented silence, leaning against the pillows.

"Were you ever close with Amber?" William asks without warning.

His tone matches my quiet, reflective mood, so I answer easily. "I don't know really. I thought we were growing up. We were best friends. We did everything together. I told her all my secrets. Looking back, I wonder if she was equally open with me. I thought she was back then, but I can think of times when she kept secrets from me even as kids. She never had an... an open personality. She was a great liar, and I used to think it was funny, but she lied a lot to me too. She always wanted more than we had. I think she loved me. And I can't help but hope that, in her own way, she still does. But I don't think relationships—even sisters—mean the same thing to her that they do to me."

He's listening closely as I talk. He puts his empty coffee cup on the nightstand and reaches over to take my hand in both of his.

"I kept trying to reconnect. For years and years. So

when she finally responded and acted like she wanted to reconcile, I thought..." My voice breaks. I swallow over the lump.

"There was always this kind of hardness at the core of her. I assumed there was at least a small amount of softness and vulnerability beneath the shell, but she never showed me even a hint of it. That's part of why it was so bewildering when suddenly I could sense real softness in her. In *you*. I couldn't figure out what happened, but I liked it so much—I wanted it so much—I kept trying to convince myself there was an explanation for it."

"There was an explanation." I lean over to press a kiss on his jaw. "It wasn't her anymore."

"That never even crossed my mind. Maybe it was a major blind spot on my part, but I'd like to think no one would jump to the conclusion that a stranger had taken someone else's place. It's just not a natural assumption."

I can't help but giggle at that. "No. It's definitely not. It wasn't a failure of intelligence or insight on your part. There was no way you could have guessed it—not without knowing Amber had a twin."

We sit in silence for a few minutes until I finish my coffee and set the cup down too. Then I snuggle against him, and he wraps an arm around me. "Part of me—a tiny, naive part of me, still hopes that maybe Amber will change. That she'll want to be close to me again."

"I can understand that. I don't think it will happen, but I can understand the hope." He's mild, soothing.

"I don't think it will happen either. What are we going to do about her?"

"What do you want to do?"

I sigh. "I don't know. She doesn't know that you know the truth. I assume she's eventually going to make an appearance and demand we switch back so she can marry you and get the money in the contract."

"I'm willing to still give her money if that's what you want." He feels slightly tense. It's clear he doesn't like the idea but will do it for me.

I'm touched. I turn my head to kiss his chest. "I don't think that's a good idea. She's already stolen money from you. You said she gained access to that account. She shouldn't get any more of your money unless you freely decide you want to give it to her. I don't want you to do it just for me." I pause and admit the truth. "To tell you the truth, I don't think she deserves any more."

He chuckles. "Okay then. We agree. I haven't cut off that account because I was going to use the money trail to track her and figure out what she was up to. But if you want, I can cut it off and we can be done with her."

"And what will we do when she shows back up? What about the contract?"

"The contract allows either of us to pull out before marriage. The only payouts are after the wedding. I'll pull out and square it with my lawyers. Cut off that account she's been draining. Then it won't matter if she shows back up. What can she do?"

"Not much. I guess she could expose the situation to the world."

"She signed nondisclosure agreements. About our arrangement. We both did. If she talks, she risks getting sued."

"Well, that will help, but it might not stop her."

"Maybe not."

I shrug. "But I don't want to be Amber forever. I want to be Jade."

"So be Jade."

"I don't want you to be plastered over every gossip site and tabloid. You don't deserve that kind of notoriety."

"Neither do you."

"But it's not your fault this is happening. It is mine. I'm happy to take responsibility. I just don't want you to get a shitload of negative consequences from it."

He works his jaw for a few moments, obviously thinking. Then, "Okay. Let's think about it awhile. We can probably come up with a workable plan. And if that fails, then we can simply pay her off."

"What? You said you didn't want her to get your money."

"I don't. Out of principle. But there are a number of problems here that can be dealt with by throwing money at her." He lifts my face so I'm meeting his eyes. "Jade, I don't care about money that much. And even if I did, I have plenty. I can spare the original amount in my contract with her without blinking. So if what we try doesn't work, then we can offer her what she wants. It will be worth it to me to just have the problem taken care of."

"Okay. What... what will we tell other people when I'm suddenly Jade?"

"We can tell the truth to the people we care about, and we can tell absolutely nothing to anyone else. It's not their business that I'm with Jade Delacourte instead of Amber."

"Maybe they'll think I just changed my name."

He huffs with amusement. "They might. It doesn't matter. I want to be with Jade, so I'm going to be with her. Nothing is going to get in my way."

"Okay. Let's work on a plan then."

"Good. Then once we deal with Montaigne, we'll be free and clear to live our lives any way we like."

I smile up at him rather mistily. "I can't wait."

"So that's the whole story," I say three days later, concluding a twenty-five-minute explanation to Haley of how I ended up taking Amber's place. "As wacky and convoluted as you can imagine. But I'm really sorry I lied to you. I didn't feel like I had much choice, but I did lie."

She shrugs, her eyes wide and her mouth turned up in what looks like thrilled bemusement. "Of course you didn't have a choice! I'm amazed you managed as well as you did. I knew something was off. I *knew* it. It felt like you were a different person, and I simply couldn't understand it."

This is the first time I've left the apartment since spotting Montaigne at the park. William has arranged for security for me. My bodyguard checked out this coffee shop before I got out of the car, and now he's standing at the entrance. I don't want to live in constant fear, but I'm nervous. Things are finally working out, and I don't want a stalker to ruin everything for me. So I've been hesitant to go out in public and had to make myself meet Haley here almost an hour ago. But I want to build a life for myself that includes real friendships, so I forced myself to overcome my nerves. "I was. You were completely right. You and William were the only ones who had any suspicions at all, but I think that's because Amber was so distant with everyone rather than me having any particular knack for deception."

"Oh, you were good. But yes, Amber's life made it easier. So William figured it out a while ago and didn't tell you?"

"Right. He didn't tell me."

"You're not mad about that?"

"No. What kind of hypocrite would I be if I was mad at him for lying to me?"

She opens her mouth to object, and I can predict what she's going to say.

"I know this one thing doesn't give him an excuse to lie for the rest of his life, just like I've committed not to lie to him again. But he understood where I was coming from. Why I felt so desperate. And I understand where he was coming from too. He didn't know who I was or what I was doing taking Amber's place. And even when he started to figure out my intentions and motivations, he still..." I clear my throat, suddenly emotional. "He wanted me to trust him. He wanted me to come clean by choice, not because he forced my hand. And he was right. I needed to make that choice. I needed to trust him if we're ever going to make this work."

"He's obviously crazy in love with you. It's really very romantic."

"Haley." My cheeks warm, but I still get a thrill of excitement because I know she's right.

"Don't try to stop me from saying what's obviously true. I get it's still new to you, and you haven't had a lot of experience in good relationships. But you're allowed to admit it. You're allowed to feel safe in it."

I swallow hard and nod, dropping my eyes briefly. "I know. It is true. He loves me, and I love him too."

We smile at each other for a minute. Then her expression changes. "Thanks for telling me. For trusting me. I won't tell anyone."

"I'm not enforcing the secret. You're free to talk if you want to. We're basically just not explaining ourselves. It's not anyone's business except the people who care about us."

"That makes sense. But there is still a wild card here. What are you going to do about Amber?"

I start to tell her about the plan for dealing with Amber that William and I worked out and agreed to, but the words get trapped in my throat at the sight of a man coming out of the men's room in the back of the coffee shop.

Receding hairline. Wire-framed glasses. Expensive clothes. A smug smirk.

Montaigne.

I freeze for a few seconds, shocked and terrified. He must have been following and talked his way in through the back. There's no way he was here before or my body-guard would have seen him.

He starts walking over toward me. Smirks again. It's that expression that finally slices through my fear.

I push the panic button on my wrist. Stand up so quickly my chair falls over with a loud clatter.

"Are you okay?" Haley asks, jumping up too and clearly worried.

I open my mouth, telling myself to scream, to call for help, to do something other than back away slowly. But I can't make my throat work.

He's going to reach me in about ten seconds.

He doesn't get a chance because Caleb, my big, hand-some, dark-haired, blue-eyed bodyguard is already here, approaching with long strides, grabbing Montaigne and forcing him up against a wall.

He's talking through his earpiece, but my mind is too fuzzy to understand the words he's saying.

It doesn't matter. There's nothing I need to do.

Montaigne broke a restraining order, and now he's been caught.

That evening, I'm curled up on the couch in the media room when William gets home.

I called him immediately, but he was almost two hours away in a business meeting. He jumped into the car to get back to me, but he got stuck in a major traffic jam coming home.

He checked in every half hour, and each time I assured him I was fine.

I *am* fine.

I spent a lot of the past several hours crying, but it's more from relief and aftermath than it is from upset.

I'm not foolish enough to assume this means Montaigne is totally stopped, but this will change things. Significantly.

He doesn't get free rein to stalk me ever again.

William puts down his case and shrugs out of his jacket as he hurries over to the couch. He sits down and wraps his arms around me, pulling me against him. "I'm so sorry, sweetheart. Damn traffic. I was about to explode at the delay."

"I know you were, but I told you I was fine."

"I know. But it was still like torture, not being able to get back to you right away." He nuzzles my neck and tightens his arms.

"I know. But we had it under control. I'm glad you're here now though."

We hug for a long time, and I feel better and stronger when I pull away.

He says, "I was just talking to the DA's office. He's in custody for now, and they're going to push for a high bail because of his history with stalking."

"His family has money though."

"Yeah. But from what I've researched, they also care a lot about their reputation. Are they going to want to keep supporting someone who is such a disgrace? Maybe. But maybe not."

"I guess so." I sigh. "We'll see. But I feel better even if he gets out on bail. We'll just keep up with the security as long as he's even possibly a threat."

"Yes. And even afterward as far as I'm concerned. I'm not going to let anyone touch you."

I snuggle against him, giggling foolishly. I think it's just an overload of emotion.

We stay on the couch for a long time, sometimes talking, sometimes just holding each other. Until eventually I need to use the bathroom and William wants to get out of his business suit.

I'm walking past our closet when I hear a phone ring.

It's not my phone. My phone is in my pocket and silent. I've gotten my own now since Amber's phone never felt like mine.

The ringing is coming from the closet. Which means it must be Amber's. I've been leaving it on and charged on a shelf in there.

I step in and glance at the screen. The number is unfamiliar. I pick it up instinctively, saying, "Hello?"

"Jade."

I freeze. Suck in a sharp breath. "Amber?"

"Yeah."

We're both silent for a few seconds. Then I ask, "What do you want?"

"I heard they caught your stalker."

She must somehow be keeping tabs on me because the interaction at the coffee shop definitely didn't make the news or get a lot of publicity.

"Did you?" I'm not nervous. Not upset. It feels more like I'm caught in a numb trance.

William must hear me talking because he comes to the closet doorway and stands there motionless. Listening.

I put the call on speakerphone so he can hear both sides.

"If you're not in danger anymore," Amber continues, "I thought maybe you'd want to switch back. There's only a couple more weeks before the contract runs out, so I thought now would be a good time."

I make a weird, dry bark of laughter. "Is that what you thought?"

"Y-yes. I thought so. What's the matter?"

"You really think it's all going to go back to the way it was?"

"Why shouldn't it?"

"Because you used me. And you used William. And we're not going to be used anymore."

She doesn't answer for an uncomfortably long stretch of time. "What's going on?"

"William knows the truth."

"Wh-what the fuck? Why did you tell him?" The sweetness in her voice has completely vanished.

"He figured it out for himself. We've worked things out on our own. We're fine as we are."

"But... then... What the fuck...? What about me?"

"What about you?"

"I'm owed something. You wouldn't be where you are

without me! And I have a contract with William. You think I'm going to just walk away—"

"I don't really care what you do. William has pulled out of the contract, which is allowed at any point for either one of you. He's worked it out with his lawyer. Both of you signed nondisclosure forms, and he's prepared to enforce it, so I wouldn't advise you to go to the press with whatever story you concoct of being a victim. We've moved most of the furniture and art in the apartment that you picked out and all your clothes and possessions into a storage unit. It's yours free and clear. I've also given you half of Mom's jewelry and everything that used to be Dad's. You've stolen money from William—and he has a documented paper trail for it—but he's prepared to let that go and not press charges for it if you go away and leave us alone."

"That's it? You want me to just go away? How am I supposed to support myself?"

"You've got the money you stole from him, and otherwise you can get a job. You're an adult. You're responsible for yourself."

"But I'm your sister! How can you treat me this way!" Even now, she sounds more outraged than grieved.

"I was also your sister when you ignored my pleas for reconciliation for year after year. I was also your sister when you used my desperation against me to get what you wanted. Maybe one day I'll feel different, but for right now I don't want to see you or talk to you. I'm building a life for myself for the very first time, and it's a good one. I'm not going to let you do anything to make it worse for me."

"What about my life? Where's William? I want to talk to him."

I meet his eyes, and his mouth twitches up in the corner in almost a smile. I say, "He doesn't want to talk to you. If you cause trouble for us, he's going to press charges for the theft."

"Jade, don't you dare—"

"I'll text you the information for the storage unit. William paid it for a year, but after that, you either need to take on the payments yourself or forfeit what's inside. If you need money, there's plenty of stuff in there you can sell for cash. You're not destitute. You just didn't get what you wanted out of this scheme. It happens."

"Jade—"

"That's it. We're canceling this phone plan, and we'll leave the phone itself in the storage unit with the rest of your stuff. Do what you want with the rest of your life. Just leave us alone."

She's starting to object again, but I disconnect the call. Then I stand still, breathing raggedly.

William comes over to hug me. "Good job."

I shake against him for a minute, but I'm not crying. The truth is, I feel ridiculously proud of myself.

~

I reach into the hot oven and pull out the large pot. It smells delicious, and I hope it tastes as good as it smells.

When I place the pot on the granite counter and open the lid, I'm greeted to the sight and scent of beef bourguignon. The beef is so tender that I'm able to fork off a little bite. As I bite into it, the flavor hits my taste buds, and I do a little dance of excitement in the kitchen.

I've been working on developing a jewelry line in the past month after Montaigne's bail was set very high and his family refused to pay it. His trial won't be for a while. If convicted, the most he'll get is six months in jail, but that will at least give us some time and freedom.

Maybe when he gets out, he'll have moved on from his obsession with me.

Right now I'm not worrying about much except taking safety precautions.

Since I'm working close to full time now, I haven't had as much time to cook. So I'm particularly pleased with my ambitious culinary accomplishment this evening.

I walk down the hall to William's office. The door is cracked, so I tap on it and push it open. William never shuts and locks the door anymore.

He turns around in his desk chair and stares at me blankly. He's stressed about some sort of project for work. He's been buried in it for several days.

"Dinner," I tell him with a smile.

He glances back at his computer. "Okay. Just a minute."

I walk over to where he's sitting. "It's ready now. You can work later." If I'm not firm, his "minute" will turn into a full evening of work. He still has trouble setting appropriate boundaries when he's stressed.

He sighs, saves his document, and lets me pull him out of his chair. As we go into the kitchen to set the table and get dinner together, I ask him about his project. Since he's tired, he talks more than usual, going on at length about the details and obstacles he's trying to deal with. By the time we sit down to eat, he's relaxed and smiling. He asks me about what I accomplished today, so I can tell him about the meeting I had about branding for my jewelry line.

My beef bourguignon is a success, and I'm pleased when William doesn't immediately put his plate up and head back into his study to work.

Sometimes he still does. He'll always be an intense, complicated man and a borderline workaholic. And that doesn't change just because I love him and he loves me.

He finishes off his glass of red wine and smiles at me tiredly, his eyes unusually soft. "I should get back to work," he murmurs, still making no move to go.

I give him a half shrug and slant him a teasing look. "I'm not stopping you."

"Yes, you are." His lips are twitching a little.

"I haven't said a thing!"

"Sweetheart, you don't need to say anything to distract

me." He reaches up a hand to gently brush my hair back from my face.

I'm feeling a little sappy but decide it's all right to indulge it.

We're clearing up the table when I remember something else. "Did you see the news about Amber?"

"I did. We figured it was coming."

Last month, Amber started dating a wealthy film producer, forty years older than her. Today it was announced they are engaged. So she'll get the lifestyle she's always wanted and a man who is probably much easier to manipulate than William.

"You feel okay about it, don't you?" he prompts when I don't reply. He tilts his head so he can better see my expression.

"Yeah. I'm fine. As long as she's safe and doesn't break the nondisclosure agreement, I don't really care what she does. It would be nice if we could be close again, but I guess that will probably never happen."

"Probably not." He steps over so he can hug me, pulling me against the length of his body.

His embrace is warm and soothing. It fills me. He fills me.

He makes everything better.

"I don't imagine she's really happy, but maybe she's satisfied at least," I finally say, pulling away from him enough to look up but still holding on to his hips. "I hope so."

His eyes soften on my face.

"What?" I'm a little embarrassed for some reason.

"Nothing." He leans over to kiss me briefly as I lean against the kitchen sink. "I just like to see how big a heart you have."

"Well, she's my sister," I mumble, almost defensively.

"I know she is." He wraps his arms around me again. "I know she is."

When we pull apart, William says, "Okay. Now I really do need to get a little more work done."

"That's fine. I'm going to take a bath and relax some. But just keep in mind that I'll be expecting you in bed before too late tonight."

"I won't forget."

"I mean it. I'll come get you if you work too late, and I'll drag you to bed if I have to."

"I never doubted it."

I love the dryness in his tone and smile at him rather besottedly. "I love you, William. You know that, right?"

"I do. Conveniently, I love you too."

William is smiling as he returns to his office, and I'm smiling as I finish putting up the leftovers of my delicious meal.

Six months ago, I took my sister's identity out of desperation and met William Worthing for the first time in the guise of someone else. It's hard to wrap my mind around how different my life is now.

William and I both spent most of our lives believing we'd never be anything but alone, and now we get to spend our forevers together.

EPILOGUE

Five months later, William and I are sitting on a bench in the park near our building.

It's been a leisurely Sunday so far. We slept in, had some slow sex filled with laughter and cuddling, and then finally got dressed and walked to our favorite brunch place.

We ate a lot and drank mimosas and then spent about a couple of hours wandering around and looking in shops until we ended up here, sitting on our favorite bench in the park.

Caleb, our primary bodyguard, is positioned several feet behind us. He's big and stoic and blue-eyed, and I've slowly been able to uncover a hint of his real personality behind the professionalism. At the moment, he's all business, perpetually scanning our surroundings with an intimidating stance that causes random passersby to find detours around us.

Vince Montaigne is in prison for a couple more months, so there's not likely to be danger at the moment. But William refuses to take any chances, and I can't say that I mind.

After so long living in fear, having an ever-present bodyguard is a luxury rather than an intrusion.

William is so protective that sometimes I wonder if he's planning to make the bodyguards a constant for the rest of our lives.

I like that he's protective. If I had a problem with any of his choices, I know I could tell him and he'd listen. But the close protection isn't a problem for me, and I know it makes him feel better just like it does me.

He's got his arm draped around me, and I'm pressed against his side. I glance up at his face and unexpectedly meet his gaze. His expression is soft. Relaxed.

He hasn't looked at his phone or email since first thing this morning. He'll always have workaholic tendencies, but he's slowly learning to relax more. Not just on the weekends but also in the evenings. Only once in this past week has he gone to his home office to work after dinner.

Every small victory makes me happy.

I've been idly rubbing one of his thighs. Eventually, William gently lifts my hand and holds it.

At first, I wonder if my touch was accidentally getting too intimate for a public park, but then I see he's studying the bracelet on my wrist.

It's a new one. I just finished it a couple of days ago, and it took me a long time to craft. Because I always intended it for myself rather than the special line of jewelry I'm developing for the Worthing retail line, I've been working on it only on and off for the past few months. It's made up of intricately designed links studded with jade stones.

I should have known William would notice it. He notices everything about me. It's been an entirely new experience for me to have someone care so much that no small details about my mood or appearance goes overlooked.

"This is gorgeous," he murmurs, lifting my wrist higher so he can study the bracelet more closely. "Why didn't you tell me you finished something new?"

"It's just for me. Not for the Delacourte brand."

"If it's for you, then I'd care about it even more." He gives me a fondly impatient look. "I love it."

"Thank you. I guess I just wanted to do something for myself. To celebrate..." I give a little shrug. "How far I've come or something. I didn't want to make a big deal about it."

He lifts my hand so he can kiss the underside of my

wrist, just above the bracelet. "It doesn't have to be a big deal to anyone else, but you're a big deal to me."

Feeling like melting, I stretch to press my mouth against his. "You're the biggest deal that's ever happened to me."

He chuckles at that. "Same."

He's still got a hold of my hand, studying the bracelet and stroking my fingers. Eventually, he starts focusing on my ring finger, on which is a lovely emerald-cut diamond he gave me with a proposal two weeks ago.

I said yes to the proposal, of course. Nothing will make me happier than marrying him. We've even got a wedding date set nine months from now.

Occasionally, it crosses my mind I'd like to tell Amber about our engagement. We haven't made it public yet, so she won't know. She's called me a couple of times in the past month, rambling into my voice mail about how she's sorry, how she wants to reconnect, how she wants her sister again.

I haven't returned her calls. I don't know if I can trust her. But I'm thinking about taking a tiny experimental step to see what happens.

I haven't decided yet.

William kisses my ring finger just above the diamond. I smile up at him, sappy and relaxed.

I'm not in any hurry to move, and William clearly isn't

either. We stay in the park for nearly an hour until Caleb moves close to us and asks softly if we don't mind returning home. There's someone across the lawn who bothers him.

I don't see anyone who looks remotely like a threat, but Caleb is the professional here, so we get up to walk back to our building.

Caleb has relaxed by the time we enter the lobby. He tells us it's all fine. No one followed us.

He comes up to our apartment and walks through every room before he lets us in. He always does that, even though the only access to it is a private elevator that has a twenty-four-hour guard. He gives me a twitch of a smile before he leaves us alone.

I smile at his strong back and broad shoulders as he exits. "I like him," I say casually.

"I like him too. He's good." William glances at my face and the front door where Caleb just disappeared. "Just don't like him too much."

I giggle at this and give him a soft hug. "No chance."

"Good to know." He hugs me back before he releases me. "He is a good guy though. He's worked for our family for a long time."

"Really? I never noticed him."

"He wasn't assigned to me. He was actually assigned to Louisa at first."

"Louisa, your cousin?"

"Yeah. She was really wild when she was younger, and her dad was paranoid." He huffs with amusement. "She ran the poor guy ragged for a couple of years. When she went into rehab, he got transferred to handle general security for Arthur. And then when we needed the best to protect you from Montaigne, he came over here."

"Oh interesting." I lean over to take off my shoes and leave them in the entryway. "When am I going to meet Louisa?"

"She keeps to herself now most of the time, but I can give her a call and see if we can visit for a weekend or something. She's up in a small town in Maine. She'll definitely come for the wedding."

"I'd love to visit if she's up to it. I love hanging out with Arthur and Scarlett, but it feels like I don't really know the rest of your family."

"They're pretty well scattered, but I'll work on it."

"Thank you. If they don't want it, it's fine. You don't have to push. But I'd love to get to know them if they're willing. I don't have any family except Amber," I explain, easing closer to him with my hands on his shirt.

"That's not true," he says, his brown eyes very sober. "You have me now. I'm your family."

I swallow hard, touched and melting with feeling. "Yeah."

"And maybe one day we can grow our family." His eyebrows lift in a gentle question. "Have some kids?"

I nod urgently, momentarily unable to speak. "I want that too."

His face breaks briefly before he pulls me into another hug. "All right then. When we're ready, sweetheart, we can make that happen."

ABOUT NOELLE ADAMS

Noelle handwrote her first romance novel in a spiral-bound notebook when she was twelve, and she hasn't stopped writing since. She has lived in eight different states and currently resides in Virginia, where she writes full time, reads any book she can get her hands on, and offers tribute to a very spoiled cocker spaniel.

She loves travel, art, history, and ice cream. After spending far too many years of her life in graduate school, she has decided to reorient her priorities and focus on writing contemporary romances. For more information, please check out her website: noelle-adams.com.

Made in the USA
Las Vegas, NV
16 February 2025

18216579R10146